D0139483

Never Surrender

Also by Kaylea Cross

Go to kayleacross.com for more information.

ROMANTIC SUSPENSE

DEA FAST Series
Falling Fast

Colebrook Siblings Trilogy
Brody's Vow
Wyatt's Stand
Easton's Claim

Hostage Rescue Team Series
Marked
Targeted
Hunted
Disavowed
Avenged
Exposed
Seized
Wanted
Betrayed
Reclaimed

Titanium Security Series
Ignited
Singed
Burned
Extinguished
Rekindled
Blindsided: A Titanium Security novella

Bagram Special Ops Series
Deadly Descent
Tactical Strike
Lethal Pursuit

Danger Close
Collateral Damage
Never Surrender (a MacKenzie Family novella)

Suspense Series
Out of Her League
Cover of Darkness
No Turning Back
Relentless
Absolution

PARANORMAL ROMANCE
Empowered Series
Darkest Caress

HISTORICAL ROMANCE
The Vacant Chair

EROTIC ROMANCE (writing as *Callie Croix*)
Deacon's Touch
Dillon's Claim
No Holds Barred
Touch Me
Let Me In
Covert Seduction

Never Surrender
By Kaylea Cross

A MacKenzie Family Novella

Introduction by Liliana Hart

EVIL EYE
CONCEPTS

Never Surrender
A MacKenzie Family Novella
Copyright 2017 Kaylea Cross
ISBN: 978-1-942299-84-4

Introduction copyright 2017 Liliana Hart

Published by Evil Eye Concepts, Incorporated

Author's Note

Dear readers,

I'm so darn excited to be part of Liliana Hart's MacKenzie family, and to catch up with the Bagram crew! Writing this novella felt like I was visiting with old friends, a very cool feeling for an author. I've missed these amazing guys and gals a lot.

Hope you enjoy this one. Get ready, because in addition to all the action, Ace's grandma has plenty of antics and shenanigans up her sleeve.

Happy reading!
Kaylea Cross

Author Acknowledgments

A huge thank you to Liliana Hart for inviting me to be a part of her MacKenzie World, and to the editing and marketing team behind this project.

And to my own personal editing team, for all their hard work behind the scenes. Thank you so much!

Finally, to my own dearly departed grandmother, a character in real life. This story wouldn't have been half as much fun without you in it.

Dedication

This one's for all my Bagram fans. I've missed these guys and gals so much! Our men and women in uniform are incredible, aren't they?

And, for Grandma C. You were such a character in real life, and I have a feeling you'd be tickled to see your likeness in the pages of my stories. Not surprisingly, you stole the show as much in this story as you did in real life.

Also, just so you know, we did indeed play Johnny Cash's *Ring of Fire* at your memorial service, as requested. You're welcome. Every time I hear that song, I think of you and smile.

Hope it's not too hot down there, and that there's a healthy reserve of rye. xo

An Introduction to the Mackenzie Family World

Dear Readers,

I'm thrilled to announce the MacKenzie Family World is returning! I asked five of my favorite authors to create their own characters and put them into the world you all know and love. These amazing authors revisited Surrender, Montana, and through their imagination you'll get to meet new characters, while reuniting with some of your favorites.

These stories are hot, hot, hot and packed with action and adventure—exactly what you'd expect from a MacKenzie story. It was pure pleasure for me to read each and every one of them and see my world through someone else's eyes. They definitely did the series justice, and I hope you discover five new authors to put on your auto-buy list.

Make sure you check out Spies and Stilettos, a brand new, full-length MacKenzie novel written by me. This will be the final installment of the MacKenzie series, featuring Brady Scott and Elena Nayal. After eighteen books of my own and ten books written by other bestselling authors in the MacKenzie World, it's going to be difficult to say goodbye to a family I know as well as my own. Thank you for falling in love with the MacKenzies.

So grab a glass of wine, pour a bubble bath, and prepare to Surrender.

Love Always,
Liliana Hart

* * * *

Available now!

Chapter One

Candace "Ace" Wentworth strode into the lobby of the grand resort's main building like she owned the place, which she guessed she kind of did. In a roundabout way, anyhow.

She could barely contain her excitement at being here again, because this was going to be a big week. Her husband was still overseas at Bagram, but in about fifteen minutes she'd be reunited with two of her former roommates from her deployments there—including her bestie, Maya—for the first time in a year.

Life might have taken all five of them in different directions, but they still kept in touch. Their time at Bagram and the things that had happened there had forged bonds that no amount of time and distance could break. Weddings had a way of bringing old friends together, and this particular one was going to be magical.

It felt good to be back here again, the first time since she'd enlisted. Located just outside the town of Surrender, Montana, The Hills resort was an exclusive property consisting of a sprawling collection of huge log cabin-style buildings built near the end of the nineteenth century. Ten years ago the owners—her grandmother included—had completely refurbished everything, restoring each building and the grounds to their original Gilded Age splendor.

Soft piano music drifted through the luxurious expanse of the lobby as she walked across the gleaming wide plank flooring, her high heels clicking softly. A warm glow from antique light fixtures more than a hundred and twenty-years old mixed with the natural evening light streaming through the wide, tall windows covering the exterior walls. Beyond them, pastures rolled like a green and gold carpet away from the buildings as far as the eye could see, the huge glass panes framing a breathtaking view of the surrounding hills and ranchland.

On the far side of the lobby, she turned left and followed the thick rug lining the center of the hallway that led toward the lounge, an exquisite room with wood-paneled walls and ceilings. It looked like the kind of masculine study that one of the Vanderbilts might have built at the end of the 1800s.

As expected, it wasn't hard to find her grandmother.

Candace spotted her instantly over at the long, polished bar in the corner of the room. The legendary Ruby Bradford sat on a high barstool nursing a rye, a cigarette dangling from the fingers of her other hand. Unfiltered, of course, because what would be the point of suddenly switching to filtered ones after all these years?

Given that it was almost seven, Candace guessed it was likely her grandma's fourth or fifth "drinky-poo" of the day. If not more.

"Hey there," she said.

Her grandma turned on the stool, exposing the length of her stocking-clad calves below the hem of her knee-length skirt, and raised an eyebrow. "Well, look who it is: my Candy Cane." She lifted an arm by way of invitation and Candace leaned down to hug her, trying not to cough at the cloud of smoke surrounding them.

"Good to see you." She pulled away and sat on the next stool. "I guess this means the non-smoking thing doesn't apply to you?" she said in a wry voice.

Her grandma's pale green eyes twinkled with the mischief she was legendary for. Ruby Bradford was one of a kind, and a force of nature. Anyone who tried to get in her way got bulldozed before they even realized what was happening. "Oh, poo. We're the only ones in here, so it's not like I'm bothering anyone. I just needed a quick nicotine fix. What are they gonna do, kick me out of the place I own half of?" She snorted. "I think not." She swallowed the remaining half-inch of rye in her tumbler and signaled the bartender, who'd been at the far end polishing glasses. And probably trying to avoid the smoke. "I'll have another, please, Elliot."

Candace caught the way the man tried to smother a grin as he took the glass and poured another inch of rye into it. "So, when did you get here?" Her grandma had flown in from the Hamptons, where she'd been on vacation for the past month.

"Last night. Where's Ryan?"

"He's flying in the morning of the wedding. Unless something comes up." A strong possibility, given how busy his unit had been during this latest deployment. Combat controllers were in huge demand on the battlefield.

The heavy feeling in her stomach returned. Things hadn't been going the greatest between them for the last little while. It had been months since they'd last seen each other, shortly before she'd left Bagram. She missed him so damn much, she couldn't wait for him to get here.

Even if she was dreading the talk they had to have once he did.

"I'm sure it'll all be fine." Grandma tapped her cigarette over an ashtray to knock off the ash, took another drag, then blew a stream of smoke out of the corner of her mouth—away from Candace, her attempt at a concession for her granddaughter being a nonsmoker. "The bride and groom here yet?"

Erin was a former army nurse, and Wade, a former CIA clandestine service officer, who had met back at Bagram. Their love story was intense, and one of the most romantic Candace had ever heard of. They'd been placed in a safe house together in Virginia for their own protection, which turned out not to be safe at all. Wade had eventually killed the terrorist he'd served for several years while undercover, but had been unable to locate the dirty bomb they'd been hunting for in time. After the blast he'd pulled Erin from the rubble on his own in spite of the risk of radioactive contamination, and refused to leave her side.

If that wasn't romantic, Candace didn't know what was.

Since Erin was from Montana, when she'd approached Candace about the possibility of getting married here at the resort, Candace had been more than happy to do what she could to make it happen for her old roomie. "Yes, and one other couple as well."

"What about the others?" Grandma tamped out the cigarette,

and Elliot discreetly removed the ashtray to behind the bar so she couldn't light another.

"They'll all be here before the wedding." Hopefully.

"Good. I'm told the chef's got chateaubriand on the menu at the grill tonight." She took a sip of her drink and faced Candace. "So, you've got everything planned out, I assume?"

Erin had tasked Candace with setting up a few things for everyone in the days leading up to the wedding. "Yep, got it all listed right here." She pulled out her phone and brought it up. "Nothing too structured. A few group meals, a couple of activities planned. On Thursday us girls are going to the spa for the day, while the guys go out and do…whatever it is they plan on doing out in the mountains. The next night will be the welcome dinner, when Wade's and Erin's families get here."

Grandma made a face and swirled the rye around in her glass. "I think I'd rather spend the day with the guys than go to the spa."

Candace shot her a frown and nudged her with an elbow. "Don't be like that. It'll be fun." The other girls all got a giant kick out of her grandma, and Erin had insisted Candace invite her along for the day.

She raised her eyebrows. "You ever seen a woman my age get a massage? All that loose, wrinkly skin sliding all over the place?" She grimaced and shook her head. "Bah. I'd rather go drinking and shooting with the men anytime."

Yeah, because the guys would *love* to have her high-functioning alcoholic grandmother running around with loaded firearms in the middle of their bachelor party. Good God, Grandma really was terrifying sometimes. "So then get a facial and a pedicure instead of a massage."

Grandma made another face, though she refrained from commenting this time.

"There she is," a familiar, slightly Spanish-accented female voice said from behind her.

She swiveled on the stool and let out an excited squeal when she saw two of her roomies and their men heading toward them, Maya in the lead. "Hey!"

Grinning from ear to ear, she rushed over and grabbed the former Air Force Security Forces officer in a crushing hug. Maya was shorter than her, but still all muscle and attitude. Always badass.

Some things never changed, even though there was more of a feminine softness to Maya than there used to be. "It's so good to see you guys!" Candace said.

"We wouldn't miss it," Erin, the bride-to-be, joked behind Maya. Green eyes sparkling, she spread her arms wide for the next hug.

"You look fantastic," Candace told her, leaning back to run a hand over her shiny brown waves before shifting her gaze to the tall man behind her. "Definitely prettier than the groom."

One side of Wade's hard mouth tugged up at the corner, his eyes shaded by the trademark wide-brimmed black Stetson he favored. "Well, thanks for that."

"Just calling it like I see it." She turned back to Maya. "I can't get over you! So polished."

The matron of honor grinned and fluffed her sleek chin-length, chocolate-brown bob, her pretty sea-green eyes dancing with humor. The simple black sheath dress fit her athletic body like a glove and showed off the killer muscles in her bronzed arms and legs. "I know, you still expect to see me in ACUs all the time."

It was a stark contrast from the tough, tomboyish woman she'd met back at Bagram. "You look like a Bond girl."

"Hey, I like that description," Jackson, Maya's husband, said in his slight Texas drawl, stepping up next to Maya to snake an arm around her waist and nuzzle her hair. Candace adored him, and his and Maya's story was epic. "FBI Special Agent Maya Thatcher, Bond girl." After the harrowing ordeal they'd been through together as POWs in Afghanistan, Maya had applied to and been accepted into the FBI, with a glowing letter of recommendation from the Secretary of Defense. The least he could do, since she, Jackson, and Wade had saved the man's life.

Maya bumped him gently in the ribs with her elbow, the way her lips curved upward telling Candace she was pleased by the comparison. "That's right, and don't you forget it." She glanced at Candace. "Are the others here yet?"

"Not yet. Their schedules were still all over the map, but with any luck, everyone will be here by the ceremony on Saturday morning." She wished she could have a few extra days with Ryan, like the others were getting with their husbands, but a couple days together was still better than nothing. "You all remember my grandma Ruby?"

"Oh yeah," Maya said with a smirk, and shook Grandma's hand. "You're a hard woman to forget."

"I try to leave an impression," Grandma said, looking pleased by the compliment.

Candace bit back a smile. Oh, Ruby certainly left an impression all right. "So, you guys hungry?"

"Starved." Erin hooked her arm through Wade's. "And thanks again, Ruby, for comping us the rooms and helping set this up for us. We didn't expect that, but we appreciate it and it means a lot to us."

"Not at all. I'm happy you wanted to have your wedding here." She wagged her eyebrows. "And your wedding night. This mountain air is famous for working up an appetite, if you know what I mean."

Wade's expression froze and Erin seemed at a loss for words for a moment before she cleared her throat and changed the subject. "They have some place good to eat around here?"

"I hope none of you are vegetarians," Grandma said as she climbed down from her stool and stepped up beside Candace. "Around here it's steak and potatoes for the most part. Real food that'll stick to your ribs. And from where I'm sitting, it looks like a few of you could use several good meals while you're here," she added, giving Maya a pointed look. "This way, everyone. Follow me." With that, she turned and marched away toward the direction of the grill restaurant in the next building over, expecting them all to follow.

Erin snickered as Maya leaned in to murmur to Candace, "Your grandma's a trip."

"Oh yeah," she agreed. "Believe me, you ain't seen nothing yet." The Bagram group had been at her and Ryan's wedding last year, but Grandma had been pretty tame throughout the whole thing. Candace was pretty sure her dad had threatened his mother with some dire consequence if Grandma didn't behave.

"So," Maya said quietly to her as they fell in behind the others. "Your contract with the force is almost up."

"Yes."

Maya gave her a knowing smile. "You decided if you're gonna

re-up yet?"

"Not yet," she lied. She'd actually made her mind up a couple weeks ago, but didn't want to tell Maya before she talked to Ryan about it. She was done with combat missions, with being in a warzone and fighting her lingering demons on a daily basis.

Still, the decision hadn't been easy.

It had taken years for her to become part of AFSOC, let alone make captain and become the first officer on a Spectre gunship. Whenever she became a civilian again, she worried that it might feel like a piece of her was missing. "I'd miss my crew, and the aircraft itself if I left. I'd never get to be at the controls of a Spooky again, and that makes it hard to let go." Ryan wasn't going to like her decision. But flying wasn't the same for her now as it used to be. Hadn't been for a long time.

"I can understand that. Any thoughts as to what else you might want to do?"

"I have no idea." And therein lay the crux of the problem. Not just for her, but between her and Ryan. She felt lost and had no idea what to do next, and he hadn't exactly been there for her since he'd been on this latest deployment.

Maya blinked in surprise. "What? That's not like you. You've always got at least six different contingency plans in place."

"Not this time." She sighed and kept walking. With her background and résumé, she probably wouldn't have trouble finding a job as a commercial or private pilot. That didn't hold much appeal, though, not after flying one of the most advanced and feared gunships in the world. She wanted to do something meaningful with her life. "I can't help feeling like it's just time for me to leave."

Maya knew every bit of her story.

"After that mission where Ryan and I ended up in the mountains behind enemy lines together, flying was never the same for me. Now that I've fulfilled my contract, part of me wants to move on and do something else. Is that so wrong?"

"No, not at all." Maya shot her a sideways glance. "What does Ryan say about all this?"

She pursed her lips. "We haven't talked about it." Not really. Because he hadn't been interested in listening. And from what he *had* said, it was clear he didn't get where she was coming from. At *all*. She was hurt and angry that he couldn't—or wouldn't—see her side of things.

She'd forced herself to drop the whole issue for the time being because she didn't want to fight while he was overseas, since there was always a good chance something might happen to him over there. It wasn't fair to either of them to argue about it while they were apart, and he needed to be focused on his job, not distracted by her or their problems. So she'd decided to shelve it until he got back stateside.

"What about you guys? You're both pretty settled now. Planning on having kids anytime soon?"

"Not for a while yet. We both love our jobs way too much." Maya waited a moment, hanging back from the others so they could have more privacy. "Bet you're excited to see Ryan when he gets here, huh?" she asked as they reached the main building's front door.

Candace thanked Jackson for holding it for her and walked out into the cool fall air. "Yeah." Just three more days. The all-too familiar buzz of nerves started in her stomach again. She couldn't believe she was actually nervous about seeing her husband again, but this time she was.

"How long's it been since you've seen him this time?" Maya asked, her high heels clicking softly on the flagstone path that linked the main building to the one beside it.

"Eight months. How long for you and Jackson?"

"Five months and eleven days. Not that I counted or anything." Maya studied her a moment. "You nervous?"

She shrugged. "I'm always a little nervous after we've been apart so long." This time it was more than nerves, however. She was a bit apprehensive, to be honest. Part of her was worried that this homecoming would be less than idyllic.

Whenever they could swing it in the past, they'd managed to steal a few days away together. Someplace quiet, away from home and family, where they could be alone and reconnect while Ryan adjusted to being out of a combat zone again.

The readjustment wasn't as hard for her because she wasn't on the ground in harm's way the same way he was during a mission. The last time they'd snuck away together, she'd noticed a big difference in him.

He hadn't slept much for those first few days he'd been back from Bagram, and he'd been withdrawn, which was totally unlike him. All part of the wear and tear on his psyche from the constant strain he was under in a warzone.

That was another reason she'd bottled up her feelings recently, not wanting to distract or upset him. She'd done her share of operations over there too, but from the sky, with the notable exception of when she and her crew had been forced to abandon their gunship that time during a rescue attempt gone terribly wrong.

It hadn't been easy for her to get past it. If not for Ryan, she wouldn't be here today.

"I get it." Maya's appreciative gaze strayed to Jackson, a few steps ahead of them, talking to Erin and Wade. "Homecomings are the best though, aren't they?"

"Yes." There was no doubt Maya was anxious to get dinner over with so she could be alone with her husband as soon as possible. Candace didn't blame her, because the long separations were hard on couples.

Sex was always the easy part though. After being apart for so many months, forging that physical connection again was the most natural. The problem was, the rest wasn't always so easy to smooth over.

As a pararescueman, Jackson was in huge demand and served frequent combat deployments to Afghanistan and other hot zones throughout Africa and the Middle East. Unlike PJs, combat controllers like Ryan were off grid for long stretches at a time, on classified missions often conducted deep behind enemy lines.

Even with her top security clearance as an AFSOC member, there were only certain things Ryan could tell her about what was going on, and no amount of phone calls or e-mails while they were apart gave her the kind of deep, meaningful connection she craved with her husband. With their conflicting views about her career, it seemed to her they were drifting apart, and it scared her.

"Don't worry," Maya said in a cheerful tone, looping one arm around Candace's waist and giving her a squeeze. "Us girls will keep you so busy over the next few days, the time's gonna fly by. He'll be here before you know it and then you guys can work everything out."

"Yeah," Candace answered as they approached the restaurant entrance. She just hoped their time together here would bring her and Ryan closer together instead of pushing them further apart.

Chapter Two

Candace's eyes flew open in the darkness when the mattress shifted and a warm, naked body pressed to hers. Her heart rate shot up as she rolled away, then a low, masculine chuckle penetrated the roaring of blood in her ears, an instant before that distinctive, spicy scent registered.

Ryan. As the wave of alarm receded, relief and joy took its place.

"Hi," he whispered, sliding one arm around her to draw her close.

Excitement punched through her. She rolled into him, wrapping her arms around his neck and smiling against his mouth as he kissed her. "Hi. Am I dreaming?" She cuddled in closer and held on tight, squeezing her eyes shut. He was here, safe and sound, and this one embrace soothed all the emotional bruises she'd been feeling.

"Nope. Want me to prove it?"

"Mm-hmm." God, he felt good. No surprise, he was already fully erect and hot against her abdomen. Arousal stirred, warming her from the inside out.

He brought his mouth down on hers and the kiss changed from slow and lazy to hungry in a single heartbeat. It felt like a year since she'd last held him this way, rather than months. He tasted like toothpaste and felt like heaven.

When he raised his head a minute later, she was breathing faster and her entire body tingled, crying out for more. "I can't believe you're really here," she whispered, running a finger down the side of his cheek, over the short, neatly-trimmed beard.

Her handsome, proud warrior. In the last picture she'd seen of him a few days ago, the beard had been wild and bushy after spending almost two weeks out in the mountains.

"Things settled down a lot so I managed to get leave a few days early. Found a flight that got me in an hour ago and drove straight here to surprise you." He leaned back slightly, his grin flashing white in the soft moonlight coming through the blinds that covered the window above the headboard. "So are you surprised?"

Her heart squeezed. "Yes, I'm so glad you're here." She had been tired when she'd gone to bed, but not so tired she should have missed the sound of the door opening or him coming into the room. He did have crazy stealth powers, however.

He huffed out a laugh and bent to find her mouth with his once more. "Missed you, Ace."

A pang shot through her. She'd been so worried that the tension inside her would ruin this moment, but everything else seemed to fade away when she was in his arms.

"Missed you too." She pulled him down and kissed him, craving the chance to lose herself in him, and sighed as everything inside her melted. Running her hands over his bare back, she frowned in concern and pulled her lips away from his. "You've lost weight." More than he normally did during a deployment. He was all muscle and bone now, not an ounce of fat on him.

"I'm all cut and chiseled for you, baby. Enjoy it while it lasts." He nuzzled her neck.

The teasing, seductive tone didn't sway her. Worried, she took his face in her hands. "You okay?" He obviously hadn't been eating his normal rations for a while. "You're not hurt anywhere, are you?"

"No, I'm fine. Now stop worrying and just kiss me, woman." He grabbed her hands and raised her arms to pin her wrists on either side of her head.

The sexy, dominant move made something low in her belly flutter. She relented and let everything else go, heart beating faster as the anticipation and desire continued to build inside her.

Her body had already come alive beneath his, craving him because it knew exactly what he could do to her, and she wanted it right the hell now. It usually took her a little longer to catch up with his physical intensity the first time after they'd been apart, but maybe...maybe right now this was enough to mend their bond that had been tested and strained with this latest deployment.

Pushing all that aside, she focused on the feel of Ryan on top of her and the delicious heat spreading through her body. She tugged against his grip on her wrists and he released her, but before she could move he looped something around them and secured it to the base of the headboard.

She gasped and craned her neck to see what he'd done, catching a glimpse of his webbed belt a moment before he cupped her cheek in his hand and turned her face back to his. In the pale moonlight his mahogany eyes seemed black, and they glittered with a raw hunger that made her breath catch.

"Don't move."

Those two husky words, spoken in that dark velvet voice, sent a shiver of anticipation rippling through her. He'd always had a dominant edge to him but he didn't let it out as often as she'd like and it thrilled her that he was doing it now.

Next thing she knew, a wave of cool air hit her as he rolled away and yanked the covers completely off them. His low, appreciative groan reverberated through the stillness when he saw her naked body stretched out before him, his for the taking. "God, I've been dreaming about this for months. Wanna just eat you up," he murmured.

"Yes, please."

He chuckled, his beard tickling her neck as he leaned in to settle his mouth against the spot between her neck and shoulder that always lit her up like the Fourth of July. She shivered and bit her lip. Already hard from the cool air, her nipples beaded even tighter, her toes curling as that wicked mouth nibbled and sucked on that sensitive spot.

Her eyes closed and she consciously relaxed, surrendering to the moment and whatever he had planned for her. Being restrained this way was exciting and a little unsettling, but being unable to move forced her to just let go and enjoy whatever this sexy alpha male did to her.

His rumble of approval at the way she relaxed brushed over her senses like a caress, then the warmth of his hands began to glide over her body. The combination of that possessive touch, mixed with the nip of his teeth and the stroke of his tongue had her wet and trembling within minutes.

More, she urged him silently, arching her back. She'd been fantasizing about this for months, the things he would do to her and the things she'd do to him when he was finally home again.

Those big, strong hands cupped her breasts, squeezing gently while his beard pricked and tickled her feverish skin, his mouth coming ever closer to her tingling nipples. He made a low sound in the back of his throat and carefully took one bud between his teeth, holding it prisoner while he lashed his tongue against it.

Candace groaned and strained against the bonds holding her prisoner, desperate to push into his mouth. Ryan responded with a deep chuckle and sucked the captive nipple between his lips. Pleasure streaked through her, molten and intense.

Sensation spiraled outward, connecting to the incessant throb between her legs, increasing the empty ache. She moved her legs restlessly, trying to open them wide enough to wind around his hips and pull him to her. More. She needed more.

Ryan ignored her and the whimper that left her lips, clearly intending to drive her out of her mind. He licked and sucked at the first nipple, then switched to the second while his free hand coasted down her belly to the rise of her hip.

His fingers glided across her skin like the stroke of velvet, trailed over the length of her thigh and back up the inside, stopping just short of where she wanted them. He knew her body so well, knew exactly how to make her ache, how to make her go blind with pleasure.

When he decided she was ready.

She groaned in frustration and raised her hips, but he just curled a hand around one and stilled her. "Ryan…"

"I'm still hungry," he whispered against her breast, holding her gaze for a long moment before planting a trail of hot, wet kisses down the center of her body, pausing at the top of the triangle of dark blond hair between her legs.

She was so wet and swollen already, dying for him to stop tormenting her.

Releasing her hip, he reached up both hands to play with her sensitive nipples, the warmth of his breath against her mound making her heart pound and her throat go dry. "Have you missed feeling my tongue between your legs, sweetheart?"

"Yes," she gasped out, not even bothering to deny it. Deployments were long and lonely. She'd touched herself many times while imagining it was his hands, his mouth on her skin instead. He made her so damn desperate, seemed to revel in destroying the control she prided herself on.

His teeth flashed white as he grinned. "Then lie still and be a good girl while I make you come."

Oh God... Her hands clenched into fists, the breath leaving her in a pained groan when the heat of his mouth settled against her aching core. His lips covered her swollen folds, that warm, wicked tongue flicking, teasing.

One strong hand locked on her right hip to hold her still as he crouched between her legs, his tongue driving her to the brink of madness. Soft, wet strokes around and against her swollen clit that made her tremble, then thrusting inside her to momentarily soothe the empty ache before withdrawing and repeating it all over again.

Again. And again. Over and over, until she was nothing but a trembling mass of sensation.

She lost track of time as she lay there, bound and helpless beneath him, while he teased and tasted her to the edge of orgasm. Her hands found the bottom of the wooden headboard. She clenched her fingers around it and held on tight, breathless and desperate for an end to the beautiful torture, little whimpers spilling from her.

"Ryan, please..." she finally managed, panting, her heart thundering out of control.

He looked up the length of her body at her, his dark eyes smoldering with a blend of satisfaction and need that shook her to the core. Slowly, deliberately, he flattened his tongue and licked up the length of her swollen sex, pausing to swirl around her clit.

Her eyes slammed shut, all her muscles tensing as the release she craved suddenly came within reach.

Then he was gone.

Her eyes flew open, a disappointed gasp in her throat. Before she could utter a single protest he was fisting the length of his rigid cock as he moved between her legs.

Face set in harsh lines of need, he braced one hand beside her face and settled the head of his erection against her slick folds. "You're mine," he rasped out, and something in his tone tugged at her heartstrings, made her wish her hands were free so she could hold him, reassure him that yes, she was and always would be his.

The words she'd been about to speak died in her throat as pressure and heat filled her. He was so thick, so damn hard, filling every inch of her, taking away the empty ache. She moaned and set her feet flat on the bed to roll her hips. Ryan fisted one hand in her hair and bent to cover her mouth with his as he thrust deep.

She cried out, his deep growl smothered by the kiss. She tasted herself on his tongue as he drove it between her lips, the erotic act pushing her arousal even higher. The hand in her hair held her head still, his weight pinning her to the mattress.

Breathless, she wrapped her legs around his, increasing the friction between their bodies each time he moved. Every thrust and withdrawal dragged the length of his cock against the sweet ache inside her.

Whimpering into his mouth, Candace gripped him tighter with her legs and pushed up harder, desperate for more. Ryan slipped his free hand between them and settled his thumb over her clit, giving her the exact friction she needed to send her soaring.

The muscles in her thighs and belly shook as she rocked up and down in counterpoint to his thrusts, each one harder than the last. Ryan took her hard, pillaging her mouth and body as he drove them both up to the peak.

She ripped her mouth free, her head tipping back on the pillow as she started to come, her needy cries echoing throughout the quiet room. He nipped her jaw, a low, shaky groan ripping free of his chest as he plunged in and out of her, then thrust deep and stiffened, his big body shuddering hard as he groaned her name.

She lay there panting beneath his heavy weight, eyes closed as the world seemed to spin around her. After a few minutes she registered the rapid beat of his heart against her chest and the sticky sweat that glued them together. The quiet hum of the air conditioning unit gradually penetrated the ringing in her ears.

She licked her lips. "Undo my hands so I can touch you." She was starved to feel him under her hands, stroke him all over. He loved it as much as she did.

He lifted up on one arm and reached past her to untie her wrists with three moves. The moment she was free, she wrapped her arms around his broad, damp back and hugged him as hard as she could. Maybe things weren't as strained between them as she'd feared. She desperately wanted everything to get sorted out, to feel as close to him emotionally as she did physically in this moment, but not now, because she didn't want to ruin it.

"That was a memorable hello. Don't think I'll be forgetting it anytime soon," she murmured, stroking his hair, his wide shoulders.

His chuckle gusted against the side of her neck. "Good." He sighed, his entire body relaxing in her embrace, and that show of trust from such a strong man turned her heart over.

She kissed his temple. There were so many things they had to talk about, but they could wait a little while longer. They would get through the transition in her career, just like they'd gotten through everything else.

"Tired?" she whispered.

"Yeah." He rolled them onto their sides, cradling the back of her head to keep her cheek to his chest while he wrapped his other arm around her hips, locking her to him. "Love you, Ace. Glad to be back home."

Something in his tone hinted that this deployment had been extra hard on him, and she got the feeling it wasn't just because of their fight. It made her even more glad that she'd bitten her tongue while he'd been away. "Love you too." She dragged the covers up over them and snuggled into his warm, hard body.

Within minutes his breathing grew deep and even and his muscles twitched, telling her he was already asleep. Content as she was, a strange, bittersweet sadness filled her as she held him.

She was nestled in her husband's arms, his heart beating beneath her cheek, but as wonderful and intense as the sex they'd just shared had been, it hadn't fully erased the hurt she felt. They only had a few days together before she was due back in D.C. and he returned to Bagram. Before that happened, she intended to bridge the emotional gap between them in the remaining time they had left together.

Get out of your head and savor this. Savor him.

Shoving the worry aside for now, she concentrated on the feel of Ryan next to her, telling herself it was stupid to feel lonely when he was holding her so close, his grip tight and protective.

They would fix everything in the next day or two, and be stronger for it as a couple going forward. The important thing was that he was here safe in her arms, and far away from anything that could hurt him.

Chapter Three

When his phone rang, Eric woke from the light sleep he'd allowed himself to fall into. He snapped on the industrial-style lamp next to the drop-down bunk bolted into the concrete wall and squinted at the call display in the sudden brightness.

It was Lyle, his second-in-command. They both used specially encrypted phones that were changed every other day, to limit the chance of detection.

"Yeah," he answered, scrubbing a hand over his thinning hair. It was long. Too long. He needed to trim it soon, as well as shave.

The connection was muddled, something they were well used to by now, but Eric understood Lyle's words perfectly. "I just got off a call with the guy in Colorado. He's in."

A slow smile curved Eric's mouth. He'd been trying to recruit the man for months now, another step in his efforts to build his network around the country. Right now his powerbase was Montana and it spilled over slightly into Wyoming and Idaho too, but that was all about to change soon. "Excellent. That's good news."

"I didn't want to wait until morning to tell you."

"Understood. What about tomorrow's training exercise?"

"We've reconnoitered the campsite and it's still clear of any eyes and ears. Exercise is a go for oh-three-hundred. That gives us plenty of time to clear out before sunrise."

Good. "You've got the suppressors and night optic devices?"

"Picked them up this morning from the manufacturer."

One of their members was a skilled gunsmith. A handy thing to have, because trying to buy that many suppressors would have raised too many red flags and brought heat Eric couldn't afford. "How many members are attending the training?" More of an evaluation, really.

Their membership had doubled in the last four months, and was now in the low hundreds. With the volatile political climate being the way it was, Eric expected that to keep growing at an exponential rate.

Every single member had to be carefully screened first, of course, before being admitted into the organization. For security reasons, no one but Lyle and a handful of others had ever seen him. Eric preferred to work behind the scenes, recruiting and organizing. Only when the time was right would he reveal himself to his followers, who knew him only as The Captain.

"Around forty or so for this exercise. We didn't invite the entire Montana membership, to keep the numbers down in case anyone sees or hears anything."

"That's fine. Make sure to sanitize the area after, the way we planned." Standard operating procedure for his organization, to limit the amount of evidence left behind after a live-fire training exercise. Right now they had to be even more careful, so certain other measures were called for.

"Of course. Darryl said he delivered another shipment of supplies to you this afternoon?"

"He did. We're set for another six months here, maybe longer if we ration it more carefully." Eric glanced around the room he slept in.

Utilitarian. Cold. Devoid of any pictures or memorabilia that would give anyone a clue to his life or background. Only his weapons, ammo, and stockpiles of supplies were down here. If any Feds did get suspicious, start sniffing around, and actually find this place, he wanted them to think he was just some crazy prepper, obsessed with readying for the end of the world or whatever.

But he wasn't crazy. Although he *was* prepared for the end of the world, in a sense.

The end of the U.S. government was coming, sooner than anyone imagined. It would unleash a firestorm of chaos and anarchy, and he would be ready. When the flames of destruction finally died out, he'd be ready to take his place in the new, less corrupt and more just order that would rise from the ashes.

The American people were tired of the broken system they were trapped in. Eric was going to help liberate them all.

"I want an in-person report about the exercise once you're done," he told Lyle. "I need to know who's ready." The first planned attack was only weeks away, and he wasn't moving the timeline back again. He'd take the best members, carefully screen and vet them, and choose a handful from their ranks to carry out the coming operation.

"You got it, boss. See you in a few hours."

Eric ended the call and turned off the lamp before lying back down on his bunk. For more than three years he'd lived here pretty much alone, totally off the grid except for encrypted phone calls and when occasional travel was necessary to get where he needed to be.

He never used the same fake ID twice, and always took a bodyguard with him when he left the safety of his headquarters. Couldn't be too careful these days, not when the government was looking for him.

It might be pitch dark in here but he didn't need to see to navigate around as he slid off the bunk and made his way to his bank of computers. He knew every inch of this place by heart. All the nooks and crannies, the location of each weapon or food stockpile he had, every last secret the place had to offer. Just in case.

Sacrifice was a necessary part of the path he'd embarked upon. His entire life was underground now, until he made his triumphant return to the surface when the right moment came.

* * * *

"Seriously, you don't have to come down if you don't want to. I know you're still exhausted."

Ryan looked up at his wife, surprised.

Candace shot him a sardonic look, hot as ever as she came out of the bathroom with her golden hair pinned up, wearing a black strapless cocktail dress and a pair of red high heels that gave him plenty of ideas about how they should spend the rest of the evening together—alone, with the ends of those sexy heels digging into his naked back.

"And let's be honest, we all know how much you dread being in the same room as my grandma anyway," she added.

Okay, something was definitely up. They'd been apart for months, with only a few weeks together after his previous deployment. He'd assumed she'd want to spend every moment they could together, but she'd just told him he didn't have to come to dinner. What was up with that? "Something wrong?"

"No." She turned toward the mirror over the vanity to put on lipstick, and the tension in her shoulders, combined with the way she avoided eye contact with him, were dead giveaways.

Something was bothering her. He tried to think of what she might be mad at him about, but came up blank, other than one particular phone conversation a few weeks back. She tended to hold onto things longer than him though. "What is it?"

She sighed and set the lipstick down on the counter. "We'll talk about it later, after dinner."

Oh, awesome. He barely refrained from muttering it under his breath. That remote tone, and those hated words meant whatever she had to say wasn't going to be pleasant.

He repressed a sigh. A moment ago he'd been looking forward to hot, kinky sex the minute they got back to the room, while she wore nothing but those high heels and a sensuous expression. Now he was bracing for a fight instead, and that sucked.

Rather than push her and risk making things worse, he let it go for the moment, but this turn of events was a total letdown. "Fine." He couldn't keep the annoyance out of his tone. He hated it when she held onto stuff, had been looking forward to spending this week with her, which was why he'd pulled every damn string he could to get here today.

His visit had gotten off to such a promising start, too. After she'd woken him up this morning with her mouth in the best way possible, Ryan had practically been in a coma ever since. He'd slept the entire day away, until she'd woken him a half hour ago at six-thirty. And not for sex, unfortunately, but to slap his bare ass, shove a granola bar and a banana at him, and order him into the shower because they had to meet everyone for dinner.

"So, you sure you still want to come?" she asked.

"Yes." While it was true that he would give his right nut for sex, another few hours' sleep, and the chance to avoid the crazy blue-haired woman who'd slapped his face off during their first introduction a little over a year and a half ago, he had limited time here with his wife.

He wasn't going to waste any of it, whether she was annoyed at him or not.

"And just so you know, the old bird's kinda growing on me." Ruby had been shockingly well behaved during their wedding, so now that he'd made an "honest woman" out of Candace—Ruby's words—he figured she wouldn't try to hit him or anything tonight.

"Sure she is," Candace said dryly as they stepped out into the carpeted hallway outside their suite.

"What did you do all day, anyway?" he asked to change the subject as he reached for her hand in an effort to put things back on an even footing between them again.

He'd thought it strange that she'd let him sleep all day. Usually when they managed to be together she was as eager as him to spend every moment with each other. It bugged him that she'd been trying to avoid him and whatever confrontation was brewing.

"Hung out with Maya and Erin mostly. Sat around the pool and talked, had lunch. I came up to check on you after but you were still asleep and I didn't wake you up because I could tell you needed the rest."

Her tone and expression weren't annoyed, but she definitely had something on her mind. Had to be that phone call a couple weeks back. They'd bickered a little over something stupid, he couldn't even remember what now, and she'd been kind of cool with him afterward.

It had been his fault. He'd been dead tired after being out in the field for the better part of three days, and had been short with her. He'd apologized the next time they'd talked, but maybe she wasn't over it yet.

Downstairs he took her hand again as they exited their building and crossed the lawn via a flagstone path to the next one over.

This resort was classy and for the filthy rich, so he was glad Ruby had pulled some strings behind the scenes and comped all their rooms, because a stay here would have cost them an obscene chunk of their military wages. Candace came from money and while it made him a little uncomfortable still, at least none of her family held it over his head.

The lobby was busy with guests checking in, and others sitting around the large stone fireplace in the center of the room with coffee or happy hour drinks. Maya and Jackson were waiting there with Erin and Wade.

He'd served overseas with Jackson but didn't know Wade that well. Ryan liked the former spook well enough, though, and Wade was good to Erin, so he was glad he'd been able to make it here for their wedding.

"Where are Cam and Dev?" he asked after doling out handshakes to the guys and hugs to the ladies. The PJ and his former army helo pilot wife, Devon, had already checked in when he'd arrived last night. Of all the Bagram guys coming to the wedding, Ryan was closest to Cam, because they'd served over there the longest. They'd gone through hell together a few times and lived to tell about it. There was nobody Ryan trusted more to have his back, except for his wife.

"Guess they must have lost track of time," Wade said with a wry smirk.

"Lucky bastards," Ryan said, snaking his arm around his wife's waist to give her a squeeze, still hoping to smooth things over.

Her curves never failed to turn him on. She was lush and ripe and soft in all the right places. He'd rather be upstairs losing track of time with her right now too, instead of down here and dreading arguing with her later.

He was proud as hell of the wakeup call he'd given her last night, but this morning had been nice too. Slower. Sweeter. And yet he could feel her distancing herself from him now that they weren't in bed together. He pulled her closer, determined to put an end to it.

"Did everybody get the itinerary I sent last night?" Candace asked, leaning into him as she slipped her arm around his waist. That simple gesture eased some of the tension in his shoulders.

"Yep. Us guys have to be back from our trip by Friday afternoon, in time for the welcome dinner," Jackson said.

"And don't be late," Erin added, poking her husband-to-be in the chest. "Our families will be here by then, so everyone will want to see you. Us, together."

"Wouldn't dream of it," Wade answered, his lips twitching.

"We should go," Candace said, glancing at her watch. "Don't want to keep Grandma waiting."

Jackson grinned. "No, we wouldn't want that."

Ryan shot him a look. "Trust me, man. You don't wanna mess with Grandma, especially if it means keeping her from a glass of rye."

Candace huffed out a laugh and tugged on his hand to get him moving. "She's not that bad."

As a group they crossed the lobby's polished plank floor and walked toward the back of the building where piano music drifted out of the lounge. Someone was singing, someone without formal training by the off-key sound of it, and judging from the clapping and cheering going on inside, it wasn't your average piano bar music happening in there.

"Sounds like there's a party going on," he said. They were supposed to meet Ruby for a quiet drink before dinner.

"Yeah, it does," Candace agreed with a frown.

A lineup of people waited at the lounge entrance, all wearing sport jackets and cocktail dresses. Ryan angled to the side and craned his neck to see what was going on in there. Once he did, he did a double-take. But no, his bloodshot, sleep-deprived eyes weren't playing tricks on him.

Grinning, he turned to the others. "You won't freaking believe this. Or maybe you will."

"What?" Candace pushed past him as the others maneuvered for a better look.

Two people at the head of the lineup entered the lounge, clearing a line of sight just as a raucous round of applause and whistles broke out. When Ace saw why, she gasped, both hands flying to her mouth. "Oh my God, Grandma…"

"Grandma?" Maya shoved past him to see.

And yep, there was Candace's eighty-something grandma,

wearing a glittery gold evening gown—sprawled out on her side atop the piano in what Ryan guessed was supposed to be her attempt at a pinup pose.

Her short blue-white hair was curled tightly against her head, and she had a cigarette in one hand and a drink in the other. She raised her glass in a toast to her approving, captive audience, then signaled the pianist and launched into the next song, her slightly off-key voice ringing off the wooden beams in the ceiling.

The audience seemed to be loving the hell out of the spectacle, and so did everyone in their group, except Candace. She groaned and hid her face against Ryan's shoulder. He patted her back in sympathy even as he chuckled and pulled out his phone to record the show. This was too freaking awesome.

"Hey, what's going on?" a familiar female voice said from behind them.

Ryan looked over his shoulder and smiled at Devon and her husband, Cam, as they walked up. "Hey, good to see you." He shook Cam's hand and slapped his buddy's shoulder.

"Wow, Dev, you look fantastic!" Candace exclaimed, throwing her arms around the former army Blackhawk pilot.

"Civilian life," Dev said with a shrug, her black hair now grown out to shoulder length. "What can I say, it agrees with me."

"I'll say it does." There was something wistful in Candace's expression as she said it.

Ryan nodded at the Seattle Seahawk scarf artfully wrapped around Devon's neck. "Nice scarf. Guess you're looking forward to watching their first home game on Sunday?"

"I can't wait," Dev said, her gray eyes sparkling. "You can dress me up in a fancy outfit and put me in high heels, but I'm still a tomboy at heart."

"A crazy hot one," Cam told her, his arm around her waist.

"Please, I don't believe her," Candace said to him. "I know she misses flying the 60s. Tell me the truth."

Cam gave his wife a gentle smile. "You totally miss it."

Devon smiled back at him. "Maybe sometimes. But my pay and benefits now as a private pilot are a helluva lot better than what I made in the army. It just sucks that you and I are so far apart all the time now."

Yeah, Ryan knew exactly what that felt like. Deployments were damn hard on relationships. Which was why the time together as a couple when they were stateside was so precious.

"We're gonna make up for lost time this week," Cam promised, giving her a squeeze.

"Us too," Ryan said, hoping to start that right after he pried whatever was bugging Candace out of her once they got back to the room. "And to answer your earlier question," he said to Devon, "*payback* is what's going on in there." He tipped his head toward the off-key singing.

"Is that your…grandma?" Dev asked Candace, eyes widening as she peered into the crowded room.

She made a strangled sound. "Unfortunately, yes."

Cam chuckled and shoved his hands into his pockets, blue eyes twinkling. "That's awesome."

Ryan nodded and returned to filming, intent on capturing every moment of this. "For real. Especially once it hits YouTube."

Candace gasped and swatted his arm, trying to grab the phone from him. "You wouldn't."

"Oh, baby, you know I would." Damn, this was fun, and he was glad the mood had lightened between them.

"Ryan…"

He stopped recording and turned to capture her chin in his hand, leaning down to smother her protests with a smacking kiss. "I love it when you say my name like that, all stern and bossy."

She swatted his arm. "Behave." But he caught the flash of hurt in her eyes when she turned away to talk to Erin.

He smothered a disappointed sigh. Okay, he was definitely not off the hook then.

Looked like they were going to have to hash things out after all. And rather than being impatient to get her alone in their room again, he suddenly found himself hoping this dinner would go on all night.

Chapter Four

"You look so hot in a cowboy hat." Candace looped her arms around his neck and lifted up onto her toes to drop a light kiss on his mouth.

"Yeah?"

"Mm-hmm. And your beard makes you look the part even more."

She liked it when he grew a beard, which was pretty often for his job, and he loved rubbing it all over her naked body.

Grasping her hips, he pulled her into his body. "Mmm, maybe I should skip the hunting trip and stay here with you."

Things seemed better between them today, and that was a relief. He'd expected her to say the dreaded words "we need to talk" as soon as they'd come back to the room late last night, but she hadn't.

Instead she'd curled into him when he'd pulled her onto the bed and taken everything off her but those sexy red heels, and she'd been anything but cool with him after that. Afterward, holding her in the darkness as they drifted off to sleep, he hadn't brought up the issue, because hey, he wasn't stupid.

She laughed, the husky sound going straight to his groin. "You'd rather get a facial and pedicure?"

"I'd rather tie you to the bed again and make you come over and over."

She raised an eyebrow. "Like you've been sex-deprived since you got here."

"I just can't get enough of you." His sincerity behind the words must have registered with her because her deep brown eyes softened.

"I'm glad," she murmured, and kissed him gently once more before pulling back.

She was pretending like nothing was wrong, but something was definitely still off. She'd been gone again when he'd woken up this morning, and had only come back a few minutes ago, right before he had to leave to meet the others. She was going out of her way to avoid talking about the issue between them.

That bugged him. He was getting to the point where he just wanted to confront her and get the damn conversation over with. Now wasn't a good time, though, not when he was about to go away for the better part of two days. Because if things got heated, he didn't want to leave things worse between them.

"We'd better get a move on so you can get acquainted with your horse," she said, and moved to the door like she couldn't get out of the room fast enough. Like she couldn't wait to be rid of him.

His patience snapped.

He stopped her with a hand on the shoulder and spun her around. "All right," he said, staring down into her face. They'd avoided this long enough. "What's the matter?"

Her expression shuttered and she broke eye contact. "I don't want to do this right now. Not right before you're about to head off and we won't see each other for a couple days."

Normally he would leave it, but it was driving him nuts that she was holding back. It also surprised him, since Candace had never been one to mince words when she had something on her mind. "No. Tell me what the problem is."

Her dark eyes flashed up to meet his, and a spark of resentment burned there. "Pretty sure you already know what the problem is."

Nope. "If this is because I snapped at you on the phone that time, I already apologized."

Her lips thinned, outrage flashing in her eyes. "You seriously think that's what's been bothering me all this time? That you snapped at me?"

Releasing her, he took a step back and folded his arms. "Okay, fine. Then tell me what *is* bothering you, so we can deal with it." They would resolve whatever it was, move past it, and make the most of their time here together.

"I'm not doing this right now; we don't have time," she muttered, and turned back for the door.

Her response pushed his frustration even higher. "When are we going to talk about it then? Tomorrow night after the big dinner with Erin's and Wade's families? Between the wedding and the reception? Or were you planning to wait until we were on the way to the airport on Sunday morning to talk about this?" Because as far as he could see, basically there was no good time for this discussion, and they couldn't leave things the way they were.

Her spine stiffened. She spun around to face him, her jaw set. "I don't need or appreciate the attitude. I've been biting my tongue since you got here, trying to keep things peaceful."

"Is that what you call it? Avoiding me whenever you can is keeping things *peaceful*?" He raised an eyebrow. "For who? You, or everyone else?"

Anger sparked in her eyes. "For everyone. And you know exactly what's wrong, so don't stand there and pretend you don't."

They were both strong-willed people, and neither of them backed down when they felt strongly about something. Thankfully, they didn't fight all that often. "Okay, then let's hear it."

"Fine. I want out."

He went still. "Out of what?"

"The Air Force."

What? "I thought we already decided that would be a mistake."

"No, *you* decided it would be a mistake, and at the time, I was only talking about the possibility of leaving." Her dark eyes speared his, and he was actually glad to see the anger there because it meant they were going to have this out here and now.

Her leaving made absolutely no sense to him whatsoever. "You've worked so hard to get where you are. Now you're saying you want out? To do what?"

Some of the anger faded from her gaze, replaced by a vulnerability she rarely let anyone see, even him. "I don't *know*, Ryan. That's the problem, and why I tried to talk to you about it before."

"So then why not stay in until you do? Why the huge rush to get out, lose a steady paycheck and benefits?"

"Money's not everything, Ryan."

"Easy for you to say." As soon as the words were out of his mouth he felt like a total dick and wanted to take them back.

To her credit, rather than exploding at him, she took a deep breath and let it out slowly before speaking. "Look, I know things were really tight for you when you were growing up, and I realize I had a privileged childhood. But we're both good with our money and we've saved a lot since we've been in. Financially we're fine, even if I take a few months to find another job."

"And while you're doing that, we're going to eat up a good chunk of what we've saved." She didn't understand what it was like to not have money.

She hadn't grown up living off canned goods and boxes of mac and cheese every day for months while his dad stretched the finances as far as they could go so he could still cover his monthly alimony payments and the mortgage.

She'd spent her summers at a beach house in Cape Cod, while the highlight of his summers was the single trip to the ice cream shop he'd made with his dad on Labor Day each year.

He'd be damned if he allowed them to struggle like that, even for a day.

"We need to be smart about this, save for the future, because you said you want to stay home for the first few years if we have kids." Yeah, her family was filthy rich and would probably help them out if things got tight, but he'd rather die than take a handout from them. Something she knew perfectly well and thus far had respected.

"I do, but you're not hearing me. I want out, and I've made the decision to leave as soon as my contract's done. I've already sent in the paperwork."

He put his hands on his hips. "So I get no say in this at all?" Not that he was a marriage expert by any means, but weren't decisions like that supposed to be made together?

"Sure you get a say, but that doesn't mean you get to decide what I do with the rest of my life." He opened his mouth to argue, but she cut him off. "I also want to have kids before I hit thirty-five, which isn't too far away. And I have to admit, the idea of being a single mom while you serve continual combat deployments overseas doesn't sound so awesome either."

He blinked. "What does that mean? You want me to get out too?"

"No," she said, frustration clear in her voice.

Her whole argument made no sense to him at all. It wasn't logical. "Then what? Why do you want out so bad?"

"Because I can't *do* this anymore, okay? I *can't*." Guilt punched through him at the tremor in her voice. She was one of the strongest people he'd ever known, so seeing her this upset took him off guard.

"Do what?" he asked, not understanding why she seemed so emotional about this, but she spun away and ripped the door open before he could stop her.

He rushed out into the hallway after her. Thankfully it was empty. "Candace."

She shook her head and kept going, marching for the elevator, back ramrod straight, head held high. He pushed out a frustrated breath.

Goddamn it. This was bullshit and there was no way he was letting this go until he understood what was going on.

What the hell had she meant? What couldn't she do anymore?

She loved flying the Spectre. She was proud of her job and rightly so, and wanting to leave the Air Force without a clear plan in mind was totally unlike her. He tamped down his irritation and followed her, giving them both a few moments to rein in their tempers.

She studiously ignored him as the elevator doors shut in front of them. He glanced at her profile, caught the flush in her cheeks and the sheen of moisture in her eyes.

Seeing her on the verge of tears twisted something in his chest. That's why she'd just rushed out of the room, so he wouldn't see her on the verge of breaking down.

Hating her silence and to see her hurting, he lifted a hand and brushed a soft wave of hair off her shoulder. "Hey. Why are you so upset about all this?"

Turning her head, she nailed him with an angry glare. "Because you're being an insensitive, unsupportive jackass."

He snatched his hand back. *Wow, okay then.* "I'm trying to help us stay stable financially, and planning for down the road. I'm being responsible." Because if she stayed home once they had kids, they were going to burn through their savings pretty fast.

"Yeah, well, if this has been your idea of being helpful and responsible, you can not bother from now on." She folded her arms across her breasts and moved a step away from him. Shutting him out.

It pissed him off, and dammit, it hurt too.

A second later they reached the ground floor and she stormed out of the elevator before the doors had fully opened. Ryan trailed after her, angry and baffled at the same time.

They didn't speak as they walked through the front doors. Out in the bright morning sunshine she turned right and headed across the lawn, taking a deep breath as she shook her hair back over her shoulders.

God, they were going to be at the stables in a matter of minutes and, while he didn't give a shit what other people thought, he didn't want their friends to know they were arguing. Normally she was the one who wanted to hash things out until they were resolved, but now he was the one who couldn't stand to let this go on any longer. Talk about role reversal.

Enough.

He caught up to her in a few strides, wrapped a hand around her elbow, and pulled her around the corner of the building, into a shaded area where they could have at least a little privacy.

Rather than pull away, she faced him with an almost mutinous expression. Thankfully there were no more tears in her eyes. "What?"

He shook his head once. "I don't want to fight."

She shrugged, the motion tight, defensive. "I don't want to fight either, but I can't just pretend everything's fine between us. I'm not built that way."

Yes, he knew. "Okay, then tell me what you meant before. What can't you do anymore?" The deployments? Them being apart all the time?

"The missions. The flying. The lifestyle. Everything."

He blinked in surprise. "But you love flying."

She shook her head, more hurt bleeding into her expression.

"Sometimes I feel like you don't understand me or listen to me at *all*."

He frowned. "Of course I listen to you." But she was going to need to spell this out for him because clearly he didn't understand.

"No, you don't, because I've already tried to explain this to you. I *used* to love flying. But not since that mission out there with you. I'm done. I want out, only I don't know what to do after that, and for months I've been on my own in D.C., flailing, trying to figure it all out while you're overseas, and when I do turn to you for support and advice, I get told to suck it up and stay in. Like you don't give a shit about my feelings." She blinked fast, her eyes filling with tears, and it slayed him.

What? "I never told you to suck it up."

"Pretty much. You told me what to do instead of listening and caring about how I felt."

Had he? After thinking about that for a moment, he realized that yeah, maybe he kind of had, but he hadn't meant to be insensitive. Now he felt bad for the way he'd handled this. "I didn't know it was this bad for you. Do you need to talk to someone again? About what happened?"

She narrowed her eyes at him. "I don't need therapy or a shrink to fix me, Ryan. What I'm going through is completely normal."

"Okay."

She pulled in a deep breath. "I've served my country and I'm proud of that. Proud of my service. I'm strong, I've dealt with a lot, but I need a change, and even if I don't know what that looks like yet, I expected you to at least try to understand and be supportive."

The accusation in her eyes made him wince internally.

"You make me feel completely alone, like you don't care about my feelings or what I'm going through. Do you know what that's like? To not be able to depend on the person you love the most?"

Her words slashed at him like knives. God, he'd had no idea she felt this way.

Those dark eyes held his, unflinching. "When we were trapped out in those mountains, I knew you had my back. I knew you'd do whatever it took to get me out of there. And I've been nothing but supportive of you and your career. But now, when I'm struggling and needed you, I feel like you weren't there for me—and it had nothing to do with you being overseas.

"You could still have been there for me even though you were half a world away, but you weren't. You let me down and that hurt so bad because you're my husband and I thought I could always count on you to have my back, no matter what."

Ryan stared at her, his chest constricting. Jesus, he felt like a total asshole. He barely resisted the urge to rub a hand over the back of his neck. "I didn't mean to hurt you," he murmured, feeling like shit. The next words weren't easy for him, but he said them anyway. "I'm sorry."

The hurt in her eyes faded, replaced by something that looked a lot like hopefulness.

"I didn't know you were dealing with all of that." He'd thought she was handling everything fine, had never realized the extent to which that mission still affected her. She'd seemed to bounce right back afterward and returned to work, and he'd just assumed everything was okay again. Yeah, she'd mentioned it a time or two in the weeks and months that followed, but he hadn't understood what she'd been trying to tell him.

Damn, and when he thought of her going through all that alone, feeling abandoned while he was on the second of back-to-back combat tours and they had only limited communication…

"I'm sorry," he repeated, not knowing what else to say. All he knew was he felt awful and he couldn't stand not touching her a moment longer, so he pulled her into his arms, hoping she wouldn't push him away.

To his relief she sighed and slipped her arms around his waist, easing the raw ache in his chest. "Okay. Thank you."

Relief washed through him. He hugged her tight and pressed his face into her hair, breathing in the herbal scent of her shampoo. "You can always count on me to have your back," he murmured, hating that he'd made her feel otherwise. That she'd even questioned it. "I'll always be there for you. It's just sometimes, even when you tell me things, I guess I don't always get it."

She snorted softly, her cheek on his shoulder. "Yeah, I noticed. But after the first few times I tried to talk to you about it, things started going downhill fast, so I didn't bring it up again while you were away. I didn't think it was fair to keep fighting about it while you were over there, just...you know, in case."

In case something happened to him.

He understood why she'd done it, even appreciated it to a point. She'd withheld all this until now to protect him in her own way, worried about him being distracted over there, but it wasn't worth the cost. Not when the alternative was her stewing about it all this time while he remained clueless and it drove a wedge between them.

"You don't need to protect me like that. Not from anything to do with us."

Another shrug. "It wasn't something we could resolve over the phone or by e-mail while you were gone, so I wanted to wait until you were back."

He sighed and released her, catching her chin in his hand and tilting it up so she met his gaze. "Well, I'm back. Or I will be as of tomorrow night, and we can figure everything out together after that. Okay?" They were a team.

She nodded and lowered her gaze. "Okay. Thank you."

"So you forgive me for being an insensitive asshole?"

Her lips quirked and she looked up at him again, relief and humor warming her gaze. "Mostly."

"Thanks." Firming his grip on her chin, he bent his head and covered her lips with his in a slow, thorough kiss.

She melted into his hold, opened for him. He growled into her mouth as blood surged to his groin. It had been a long time since they'd had make-up sex. He mentally calculated the time it would take to get her back up to the room and strip her naked.

Candace pulled back and gave him a wry, knowing smile. "Rain check."

Damn. He cupped her cheek in his palm, holding her gaze. "I'll do better, okay? From now on I'll try to listen better."

"Okay. I'll do better too."

He was so damn lucky to have her, and it was a relief to know she wasn't still mad at him. "I love you."

"Love you too." She hugged him tight, then stepped back and checked her watch. "We better get going."

"Yeah." He knew he was truly forgiven when she reached for his hand as they turned toward the stables. He squeezed her fingers in reply, glad they'd dealt with this.

They still had a lot to iron out between them but at least they'd gotten past this first big hurdle and once he got back he was going to make time to fix the rest of it. Candace was the best damn thing that had ever happened to him and he was going to make sure she knew she could count on him no matter what.

* * * *

The stables were a seven-minute walk from the main lodge, down a gravel pathway that wound through the gardens and around the duck pond.

Set at the top of a slight knoll, the barn-red building was as well maintained as everything else around here. Pastureland spread out behind it as far as the eye could see, disappearing down a rise that gave way to some woodland. In the background stood the mountains they would head to today.

Candace walked alongside Ryan with their fingers laced together, feeling lighter than she had in months. They still had more to talk about once he got back from the bachelor party trip—like how she felt like she came in last with him sometimes—but at least she'd gotten the worst of it off her chest and he now understood what she'd been feeling these past few months.

It was a good start, anyway, and she felt way more positive about the future than she had an hour ago.

Erin, Dev, and Maya were already gathered around the corral when she walked up with Ryan, the guys standing out in front of the barn next to their mounts. Cam lifted a dark blond eyebrow at them beneath the brim of his dark brown cowboy hat, a piece of straw sticking out of the corner of his mouth. "Lost track of time?" he said to Ryan.

"Hey, you know how it is. Gotta keep getting shots downrange, because shooting skills are so perishable. Don't wanna get rusty."

Cam laughed. "So you were busy cleaning and oiling your *weapon*, I guess?"

"Yep." Ryan ogled Candace, then gave her a leer. "Course, my fast-movers always hit the targets I lase."

She rolled her eyes at the horrible pun, actually looking forward to some downtime without him now that her anger and resentment weren't eating her up inside. "You guys are ridiculous. Go take your excess testosterone and get your horses saddled."

"You love my excess testosterone," Ryan murmured in her ear, sending a rush of tingles through her.

She did. And it felt so good to be able to joke with him again without the tension gnawing at her. "You're bad. Go." She lifted up to kiss him once more, then pushed him toward the wrangler standing with a clipboard near the barn door.

"You Wentworth?" the man asked.

"That's me," Ryan said, and strode over. Candace couldn't help but admire the sight of his butt in those jeans. Yum.

The wrangler took off his hat and scratched his head. "Got a slight problem. We weren't expecting a last-minute addition to your party. All the rest of our horses are already out for the day with other guests, and your buddies got the last of our trail horses. Only one left is that one." He nodded behind him.

Candace followed his gaze, noticing for the first time the animal standing half-asleep in the shadows the barn cast in the far corner of the corral.

Ryan did a double-take. "Wait, *that?*"

"That," the man confirmed.

"What the hell is it? A donkey?"

The wrangler's mouth twitched at the same time as chuckles broke out from the rest of the group watching. "That there's Poncho. Half American mammoth donkey, half Icelandic horse."

Ryan stepped closer, an expression of disbelief on his face, and Candace bit her lip to hold in a giggle. "I'm supposed to ride that? Up there?" He jerked his chin toward the distant mountains.

"'Fraid so. He's all we got left."

Scowling, Ryan stepped up to the corral fence and eyed the weird-looking animal dubiously, already shaking his head. "I weigh two-twenty, and it's what—a four-hour ride to the ATV pickup point?"

"Closer to five. On him, maybe more like six. Not a problem about the weight. Poncho can handle you, but we'll have to divide your gear amongst the other horses, just to be safe."

Ryan turned his head to shoot Candace his trademark *are-you-fucking-kidding-me* look she recognized well, and everyone started to laugh. His mouth tightened. "Fine, whatever." He stuck a hand over the fence. "C'mere, Poncho."

"Yeah, he's not gonna come when called," the wrangler drawled, nimbly hopping the fence and walking over to retrieve the animal by the halter on its face. "And you'll find he's pretty set in his ways, too. Real stubborn."

"Ryan's the same way, so I'm sure they'll get along fine," Candace called out. Maya snickered and Wade looked like he was struggling not to burst into laughter.

After some grumbling and signing the mandatory waiver, Ryan waited while the man saddled Poncho and brought him over. Candace slapped him on the back. "Have a good time, honey!"

He shot her a dark look and bent to accept the kiss she offered. "Yeah. Good time."

"Well, better than the little donkey you rode in Afghanistan that time, right?"

He grunted, looking none too impressed by the turn of events. When he strode over to take Poncho—who stood with his eyes closed and his long ears sticking out sideways from his head—from the wrangler, the animal's back only came up to Ryan's waist. "How's this gonna work?" he demanded, scowling again.

The wrangler grabbed hold of the stirrup. "Well, you put your left foot in this stirrup here—"

"Yeah, I got it." Jaw tight, Ryan grabbed the saddle horn, put his foot in the stirrup and hoisted himself onto the animal, his long legs damn near touching the ground.

"We'll have to adjust the stirrups some," the wrangler mumbled, and went to work shortening the stirrups. He looked so ridiculous that Candace couldn't keep from laughing. She whipped out her phone to snap pictures.

"Hey, he's a low rider," Wade commented, already mounted on his own horse, which towered head and shoulders over poor Poncho.

Of the group, he and Jackson were the natural cowboys. Both of them had grown up riding.

"Fuck off," Ryan grumbled, and shifted in the saddle. Poncho didn't so much as open his eyes, his lower lip sagging open as he carried on sleeping, standing up.

"Y'all ready?" Wade called out, checking the others behind him.

"Yep, good to go."

Wade winked at Erin. "See you in a couple days, baby."

"Have fun," she called back.

"I'm already having fun," he said, smirking at Ryan.

Ignoring him, Ryan let his inner clown out and hammed it up for Candace, tipping his hat at her as she recorded some video. God, he was adorable. "Later, little lady. Come on, Poncho. Let's ride." He nudged his heels into the animal's sides. Poncho jerked but didn't open his eyes.

"Sometimes he's a slow starter," the wrangler said, and hurried over to slap Poncho's rear with a loud *thwak*. Poncho's eyes flew open, his ears went back, and he shot off in the opposite direction Wade had gone.

"Hey, Went, wanna race?" Jackson called back, a cocky grin on his face as he followed Wade at a trot.

"We'd better stop and give him a head start," Cam said, and he and the other two stopped their horses.

Ryan shot them a venomous glare, pulled hard on the reins to get Poncho going in the right direction, and hurried after his buddies. Male laughter rang out from across the pasture and Candace was giggling so much she was having a hard time keeping her phone steady.

"Woohoo, ride that pony, cowboy!" Jackson hollered, taking off his hat and giving a loud *Yee-haw!* as he waved it around his head in encouragement, then exaggerated his drawl. "Ride'm like he's never been ridden before!"

Candace could barely see through the tears of laughter in her eyes. Maya, Dev, and Erin were all gathered around her, howling at the hilarious spectacle before them.

To his credit, Ryan held his head high as he rode Poncho past the guys, the animal's ridiculously tiny steps adding to the comedic factor. Hoots of laughter rang out.

As he pulled away from them, Ryan proudly raised one arm and held his middle finger up over his head for them all to see as he rode off toward the mountains…at approximately one-point-three-miles per hour with his boots nearly dragging on the ground.

Chapter Five

"Come on, Poncho, I know you can," Ryan coaxed in a singsong voice, nudging his "horse" in the ribs to keep him going.

He'd told the others to carry on to the ATV pickup place without him, since it was clear he'd added an extra hour to the trip. Poncho's ears pricked up and he walked faster, his hooves tramping over the grass at an endearingly fast pace, considering his short little legs.

When they crested the next hill, the hunting cabin came into view at last. "Yes," Ryan groaned, looking forward to stretching his legs and drinking a well-deserved cold beer before starting the next leg of the trip.

Poncho seemed to know the end was near too, because his head came up and he hit an all-time speed record for the trip, his little legs eating up the distance to the cabin. The others were waiting outside with the ATVs when Ryan got there and dismounted, and the wrangler from the stable was there to take Poncho, brush him down, and let him eat for a few minutes before loading him into the trailer for the drive back to the resort.

"Hey, you made good time," he said to Ryan with a grin as he took Poncho's bridle.

"He hit a new gear once he saw the cabin." He turned to his buddies. "Somebody get me a damn beer."

"I got you, bro." Jackson tossed him a cold can from the cooler.

"I'd say you've earned that," Cam said with a grin.

"Damn straight." He'd be bowlegged for a week after that endurance ride. Ryan sighed and nursed the cold brew while the others strapped their gear to the backs of the ATVs. "Please tell me I get a regular-sized one this time."

Wade chuckled and bungee-tied their two-man tent to the back of his vehicle. "Yeah, you're good." He straightened, glancing at the sky. "Sun's already starting to sink over the mountains. We need to get moving." He looked at Ryan. "We're on federal land from here on out." He'd checked prior to setting up this little trip. "You good to go?"

"Yep." He drained the beer, stowed the can, and climbed onto his ATV. The moment he started the engine, he grinned. "Oh hell, yeah, that's what I'm talkin' about." He revved it and cut a sidelong glance at Jackson. "Hey, Thatcher. Wanna race now?"

"Hell yeah, I do."

Grinning, Ryan took off toward the mountains. For the next three hours they took turns trying to outmaneuver one another, being guys, and trying to see who could spray the most mud on the others every time they hit a puddle. After back-to-back deployments, he needed this downtime with his buddies.

By the time Wade took the lead and stopped to check his compass, it was nearly sunset. "Here's good," he announced, swinging one leg over the center of the ATV to dismount. "We'll set up camp somewhere around here."

Together they hunted out a good location. Ryan had to keep reminding himself he was back home, rather than in the mountains of Afghanistan. The climate might be different here, but his combat instincts wouldn't shut off. To his body, he was still back overseas, and every tree and rock could hide either an IED or an enemy fighter.

When he stepped around a large boulder and into a small clearing surrounded by forest, he noticed something glinting on the ground in the dying rays of sunlight. As he got closer, he confirmed that they were spent casings. Nudging the ground with the toe of his boot, he uncovered more. Someone had made more than a half-assed effort to hide them, but there were a shit ton of them out here.

He glanced up at the surrounding trees and realized with a start that a large stand of pines in the distance were riddled with bullet holes. So much so that in places the dying sunlight streamed through the holes. Upon closer inspection, the entire area seemed to be littered with brass casings. "Hey, guys, come check this out."

Wade, Cam, and Jackson appeared out of the trees behind him a minute later. "What's up?" Cam asked.

"Whole area's covered with 7.62s," he said, holding up a casing. "And then there's that." He pointed to the shot-up trees. A few smaller ones were even cut in two.

Turning in a half-circle to take it all in, Jackson let out a low whistle. "Somebody's been trigger happy recently."

Wade had been moving away to the southeast. "Camp fire here," he called out from behind a stand of trees blocking him from view. "They covered it but it looks recent. Maybe used in the last couple days."

"One over here too," Cam said from Ryan's right. He used his boot to dig away some of the dirt. "Pretty big. Around eight feet across."

Ryan continued walking west, scanning the ground. He paused to drag a fallen branch aside and uncovered another fire pit. "Another one here." Lots more cartridges littered the ground as he dug the surface layer of dirt away. He turned and looked back at Wade. "How well do you know this area?"

Wade lifted a shoulder as he scanned their surroundings. "Not that well."

"Is this a common campsite, or is there something else going on here? Because that's a shitload of ammo to waste shooting at trees." Last thing they needed was to set up camp and bed down with drunk, trigger-happy yahoos around.

Wade nodded, a frown pulling at his eyebrows. "No shit."

Ryan reviewed the possibilities. People could be stupid. So it *could* be just a bunch of idiots who had come all the way out here to shoot the hell out of some random trees for no apparent reason.

It also could mean something more sinister.

This area was a long way away from anything, so remote it was accessible only by foot, horse—or mutant donkey—or ATV. Not even a good dirt bike could handle this kind of rugged terrain.

Whoever had been out here before them, it must have taken a hell of a lot of effort for that many people to come here with that amount of firepower. If someone wanted to hide paramilitary or even terrorist training or other activity, this was a good place to do it. The prickling at his nape reinforced the suspicion.

"Something sure as hell doesn't feel right." He examined the ground, bending to point at the dirt. "I count at least five different sets of prints in this area here." He drew a circle with his arm, indicating an area of about ten yards across.

"More over here," Cam said to their left.

A slight unease in Ryan's gut warned him that this so-called "remote" area might not be so secluded after all. Someone might be watching them right now. "Let's split up and check it out," he said, untying his rifle from the back of his ATV. The four of them sectioned off the hillside and spread out to search it, weapons at the ready in case anyone was still lingering around.

Half an hour later they met up again. Ryan shook his head. "Found more prints and more casings." Not nearly as many as in this area though. "Tracks led to a trail about half a klick that way." He pointed due west.

"Same," Jackson said, and the others confirmed the same as well.

The sun was already setting and they hadn't yet unloaded anything. They needed to make a decision. "You wanna stay here, or keep moving?" Ryan asked Wade. It was his party. His call.

Wade glanced around the clearing. It was the only place in the near vicinity free of rocks and giant tree roots. "I think we're good. Whoever was out here is long gone and we can report what we found once we get back to the resort."

"Okay," Ryan agreed, sweeping his gaze over the surrounding trees. His gut said they were alone, and the telltale prickle at the back of his neck was pretty much gone.

"All right, let's set up camp," Wade said, then grinned. "Time to kick back and enjoy my last few hours of bachelorhood in style."

* * * *

Eric stared at the monitor in front of him, seething with anger as he tried to make out who exactly was trespassing at the training site—the ultra-remote one that was supposed to be a secret, one that no one else should have ever found. His sensors had alerted him the moment the strangers had stepped onto his land only minutes before.

Lyle stood next to him, leaning over the desk to take a better look. "Four of 'em."

"Yeah." The angle of the camera mounted in the tallest pine tree was too high to give him a good look at their faces, but Eric could see enough, and what he saw wasn't good.

They were all big men. They all carried rifles. And as they fanned out in a search pattern, they moved with a familiar, military precision that triggered his inner radar. "I want to know who they are and what they're doing out here."

"Yes, sir." Lyle got out his radio to call one of their members, but Eric stopped him with a raised hand, gaze glued to the screen. "Let's watch them for a while longer."

The four men gathered together again to talk for a minute, then began unloading gear from the backs of their ATVs. Two of them put up tents in the clearing while another uncovered one of the fire pits made by Eric's troops. The fourth appeared to be preparing food for cooking.

Eric clenched his jaw. "You were supposed to sanitize the area."

Lyle shifted his stance and cleared his throat. "Things ran later than planned. We didn't have enough time to do more than cover up what we hadn't already gathered. The sun was coming up and I made the call to abandon the area. I was planning to take a crew back tonight and finish cleaning everything up."

He aimed a lethal glare at the man. "Too late. You've already risked our exposure."

Lyle's face turned red but he didn't argue. "I'll fix it. They don't look worried, and none of them have pulled out a sat phone or anything. Maybe we're still okay."

"They saw the casings, and the trees."

Lyle stared straight ahead at the monitor rather than meet his gaze. "I'll fix it."

Damn right you will.

A few minutes later a fire was going inside the circle of stones one of the men had cleared out. All four of them brought out folding chairs and gathered around the campfire, drinking beer as they cooked what looked like steaks over a portable grill.

"They sure don't look like Feds," Lyle said.

"They don't look like ordinary civilians, either." The image on screen suggested the men were nothing more than a group of hunters setting up camp for the night, with no clue of his presence.

But Eric hadn't survived this long by being naïve. For all he knew, they were undercover agents from some government agency, looking for evidence that would lead them to him. He'd been on the Feds' radar ever since rumors of his activity had first begun to circulate a few years ago.

Hypocritical assholes. They should have protected him, stood up for him when he'd needed them. Instead they'd turned on him and made him an enemy of the very institution that had locked him up for doing what he still believed was the right thing.

They'd never find his hiding spot, even if they put all the clues together and figured out that his militia had trained in the clearing last night. He'd been here for years without detection and wasn't about to give himself away now. All this time he'd been right under the locals' noses, and no one even realized it.

He straightened and folded his arms across his chest. "We need to take defensive measures."

Many people would brand him a traitor, or even a domestic terrorist. He didn't give a shit what others thought. He was a patriot. He loved his country more than anything, had sworn an oath to defend its constitution and fought and bled to protect it. Only to discover that the system was corrupt, and the government he'd been so proud to serve had abandoned him. Turned its back on him in his most dire hour of need to avoid an uncomfortable political situation with the Afghan government.

Fuck. Them.

Soon enough, they'd pay. His followers would carry out attacks he'd planned on government installations all across Montana.

Only a few small attacks at first. Subtle, with a pointed message. Using explosives and impersonal weapons that could be planted and detonated later, on his command. Nothing too big or ambitious to start, nothing that would tip his hand and risk his future operations. Once his scattered network here and in other states joined forces, however...

From the proverbial ashes he intended to create, a new era would begin. The true leaders would rise and wipe away the old regime, restoring this great country to the glory his forefathers had intended.

Until that day came, he had to be very, very careful.

He stared at the flickering campfire on screen, his mind whirring. "Send out our two best scouts and tell them to follow these guys. I want to know everything we can find on them. Hopefully they'll leave the area once the sun comes up, but I'm not taking chances."

"You got it. What if they don't leave?"

"Then we do what we have to in order to protect the cause." Eric watched the four men eating their dinner, certain they had military training. Killing four people was a huge risk, but it might come to that. He had to make them disappear.

For now, he'd wait and see what happened. If they didn't leave the area come sunup, he would have to do some hunting of his own tomorrow.

Chapter Six

With a yawn so big his jaw cracked and his eyes watered, Ryan bundled up the last of his gear and stowed it on the back of his ATV.

Though it had been a pretty relaxed night out here with the guys, the evidence at the site made them edgy enough to take watch in shifts. He'd taken the second one, giving him about four hours of broken sleep total, and his sleep-deprived system was having a hard time waking up this morning.

"You boys ready to roll?" Wade asked them from beside his own ATV.

"Yeah," he said as Cam and Jackson replied the same.

Truthfully he couldn't wait to get back to the resort and see Candace. And this entire area gave him the creeps. He'd scanned the surrounding trees for surveillance cameras last night before losing all the daylight and found none, but he still couldn't shake the unsettling feeling that someone was watching them. The sooner they got out of here, the happier he'd be.

"Let's head out then." Wade climbed onto his ATV and fired up the engine.

Luckily, the wrangler at the resort's stable had found Ryan a full-size horse for the return trip back from the ATV drop-off point, so he made it to the barn at the same time everyone else did.

After stretching their legs for a minute, they grabbed their gear and headed back to the main buildings to drop it off. He found Candace busy helping Maya, Devon, and Erin get everything set up for the welcome dinner in the glass-paned conservatory.

"Hey, you're back early," she said with a wide smile that flooded him with warmth, and walked over to give him a kiss and a hard hug. Their talk yesterday had obviously made her feel a lot better, so that made him feel better as well. "You guys kill anything out there?"

"Just Ryan's ego," Cam answered, and Jackson and Wade snickered.

She grinned up at him, deep brown eyes sparkling. "Aww, did my badass hubby's ego take a beating, riding poor little Poncho up the mountain?"

"My ego is just fine," he insisted. "How was the spa?"

"Blissful. After our massages we all got our nails done. Dev got a Seahawks mani-pedi, but I just stuck to plain old pink. It was so relaxing."

"Mmm, I bet I could relax you even more upstairs." Ryan bent to kiss that smart mouth again. He sucked at her lower lip, teased her with his tongue.

She hummed and opened to him for a moment, then seemed to remember they were in public and pushed him away with a smile that promised to pick up where they'd left off later. "Give us a hand moving these tables around, will you? Spa day ran later than originally scheduled, so we're tight for time."

He shot a look at Wade, who had his arms around Erin. "Told you we should have waited another hour."

Candace snorted and shoved him toward the nearest table. "Here. Start with this one."

Twenty minutes later they had everything arranged and the staff began setting the tables, so Ryan went up to the room and grabbed a quick shower. When he came back downstairs, most of the guests had arrived, including Erin's and Wade's families. After he'd made the rounds to meet everyone with Candace, he left her at their table and went to the bar to get them a drink.

"There you are."

He mentally cringed at the sound of that smoke-roughened voice behind him, and put on a smile before turning to face Ruby—who was technically now his grandma too, at least by marriage. A terrifying thought. "Hey."

"Hear you met Poncho," she said, stopping next to him and waving the bartender down.

He shot her a sharp look and yeah, that was definitely a smirk on her face. "I did, yes."

"How did you boys make out?"

"Fine. Didn't come across any game, but we did find some type of training site up there."

"What kind of training site?" she asked, falling into step with him as he made his way back toward Candace with the drinks. For once, Ruby didn't have one in her hand, apparently distracted by their conversation.

"Well, guess it could have been something else, but there were a shi—uh, crapload of spent casings on the ground and the trees were riddled with holes. That's a whole hell of a lot of firepower to waste using trees for target practice." He edged past an elderly couple he thought might be Erin's grandparents and made it to the table where his wife waited with the rest of their gang.

"Whereabouts was this?" Ruby asked, taking Jackson's chair just as he was about to slide into it. The PJ stood awkwardly to the side, between her and Maya, but didn't say anything and Ruby didn't seem to notice—or care—about her faux pas.

"West of here, in the foothills."

"Yeah, but where?" she pressed, sounding exasperated.

Candace leaned forward, winding an arm around him, and he tucked her tight into his side. "What's this about?" she asked.

She smelled so damn good. "I told her about the site we came across." They'd mentioned it to the girls while they set up the tables.

Ruby was frowning. "Be more specific."

Ryan eyed her. "You want like, coordinates or something?"

She raised an eyebrow at his dry tone, her green eyes locked on his like a laser range finder. "Yes."

Seriously?

She whacked him on the shoulder. "Come on, humor an old woman. If something like that's going on near my resort, I want to know about it."

He paused and looked around the table. Everyone was watching him, and Cam seemed to be biting back a smile. "Okay then." He pulled his phone from his pocket and pulled up the nav app he used, but Ruby made a disparaging noise and flapped a hand in annoyance.

"Not on that thing. I need a map. A real map, made of paper." She turned in her chair and glanced around the crowded conservatory. "Anyone here got a map of the area with them? An *actual* map?" she called out.

Candace winced and reached across the table to set a hand on her wrist. "Grandma—"

"It's fine, dear. Anyone?" Ruby said, a little louder this time.

A man three tables over rose awkwardly and pulled a folded map from his back pocket. "I've got this," he offered as he walked over and handed it to her. "Will that do?"

"Perfect, thanks." She looked at Ryan. "Will it?"

Withholding a sigh because he wasn't completely sure she wouldn't slap him if he didn't, he dutifully unfolded the map. Just a regular road map, the kind you got at a gas station. No good topography marks or anything like that. "Hang on a sec."

He was aware of Cam and Jackson leaning closer to take a look, and Wade walking around the table to look over his shoulder while he pulled up his nav app and accessed the coordinates. "Here," he told Ruby at last, tapping the exact spot on the map where the coordinates intersected.

She squinted and leaned farther over the map to study it. "Uh huh," she murmured to herself. "And where are we now?"

"Here," Wade said, reaching over her shoulder to put his finger where the resort was located.

Ruby muttered to herself for a moment, then raised her gaze to Ryan's. "Did any of you see a big rock formation anywhere near there? Granite, I think. Kind of looks like a grizzly bear hunched over. Sort of."

He exchanged a surprised look with Cam and Jackson across the table. "Yeah, maybe what, a half mile east of there?"

Jackson nodded, his gaze shifting to Ruby. "You know the area where we were?"

"Yes, I know the place. Our bunker was near there."

Ryan swung around in his seat to stare at her. "Your what?"

"Bunker." She gave Candace a gentle swat on the upper arm.

"Candy Cane, be a dear and go get me a drinky-poo. Your handsome man distracted me so much I forgot to get one while I was at the bar." She reached up and patted Ryan's cheek. Way gentler than she had been the last time she'd touched his face.

"But I want to hear—"

Without looking up from the map, Ruby tutted and pointed a finger in the direction of the bar. "Go."

Candace shut her mouth, gave him a long-suffering look and muttered something under her breath as she got up and left the table. Ryan blinked in astonishment. "Wow, that was impressive. Is that all I have to do to get her to do what I want? Give her a command and point my finger?"

The shiny tines of a fork appeared an inch in front of his nose. He yanked his head back and jerked his gaze up to hers, startled. What the hell?

Those shrewd green eyes narrowed on him in warning. "You even think about speaking to my granddaughter like that, I'll stab you in the heart with this thing."

Maya chuckled darkly across the table. "You tell him, Ruby."

Ruby gave a decisive nod and aimed the fork at the other guys, one by one. "Same goes for the rest of you boys. I don't ever want to hear you've been disrespecting these women."

Cam held up his hands in self-defense, dark blond eyebrows hiked up. "No, ma'am."

Ryan scowled at her. Cam was too damn polite. "I was kidding."

"Just making sure." Ruby lowered the fork and went back to the map. "Now. About this site you saw."

Wade slid into Candace's vacant seat and took off his Stetson, staring at the woman who'd just threatened to do him bodily harm with a damn fork. "What kind of bunker?"

"Secret, underground type," she said with a knowing smile that told Ryan she was enjoying herself and the attention way too much. "A system of them."

"What were they for?" Ryan pressed. There was something to this. Ruby might be a crazy old lady sometimes, but she was also sly as a damn fox.

Ruby paused and glanced around them, as if to make sure that no one else was listening in. She had everyone at the table on the edge of their seat, including him as she focused on Wade. "You're with the CIA, right?"

Surprise flickered in his dark eyes for a moment before he masked it and put on a blank expression. It was damn eerie to see, but explained why Wade had managed to infiltrate the infamous—and now dead, by Wade's hand—terrorist Rahim's network and serve as his second-in-command for years without detection. "I've worked with them from time to time in the past," he said, his tone guarded.

She snorted. "Still do, from what I hear."

He frowned, his gaze sharpening. "Where'd you hear that?"

She flapped a hand dismissively. "Around. I know people. You don't get to be my age without making important connections, young man."

Wade's gaze cut to him, and Ryan gave a slight shrug. Her son was a senator, so who the hell knew what kind of connections she had in the government?

Candace arrived back at the table and thrust a tumbler at her grandma. "Your drinky-poo. And by the way, when I asked the bartender, he told me this is already your third of the afternoon." She sidled up to Ryan and slipped her arms around his chest from behind. He reached up to rub her hand, enjoying her easy affection and the fact that she wasn't mad at him anymore.

Ruby took it with an innocent smile. "Thanks. So," she said, totally ignoring Candace's comment as she turned back to Wade, "tell me. Ever heard of Project Sentinel?"

Wade's face went dead still. "Yeah," he said slowly, searching her face as if he was either looking for something, or unable to believe what he was hearing.

Ryan couldn't stand it. "What's Project Sentinel?" It sounded really cool.

Ruby smiled and tipped her head at Wade. "Ask him. Now if you'll excuse me, I need to go have a smoke." She picked up her drink, rose from the table, and sauntered away with a swish of her hips, sipping on her rye.

Everyone looked at Wade, who chuckled and shook his head. "Talk about a mic drop."

"Grandma's favorite kind of exit," Ace said, then smacked Wade gently on the shoulder. "Come on. What the hell was she talking about, bunkers?"

His dark eyes danced with humor. "It's not classified anymore, but even if I told you, you'd never believe it."

"Try me. The drama is strong in our family."

Wade took a sip of his beer and lowered the bottle back to the table. "The CIA was growing more and more suspicious about the Soviets toward the end of WWII, so they decided to take precautions and set up an intel network across the country. It included a system of underground bunkers in remote areas that served as bomb shelters, storage facilities, and think tanks."

Candace's dark brown eyes widened. "My grandmother was part of a secret CIA program?"

"Must have been, because there's no other explanation for how she knew the program name and the bunker's location." Wade picked up his beer again, a low laugh rumbling out of him. "Your grandma's the shit."

Well, hell. Ryan tugged his wife into his lap and grinned so wide his cheeks hurt. Apparently Ruby had been holding out on them all this time.

Chapter Seven

"I can't believe your grandma was a WWII spy!"

Candace rolled her eyes at Ryan as they stepped into the elevator, hand in hand, having just left dinner a few minutes ago. He sounded so excited and impressed, but she was stressed about the possibility of Ryan and the others having stumbled across something dangerous, and because she desperately needed to finish their conversation from yesterday morning.

She wanted it over and done with, so she could fully enjoy the rest of their stay here. "So what, now you're her number one fan or something?"

"I told you, she's growing on me. And come on, how freaking amazing is that?" He chuckled to himself as he hit the button for the fourth floor.

"I'm sure she wasn't an *actual* spy. You know how she likes to tell stories, and even the real ones are embellished. Maybe she had one too many drinky-poos and decided to use a little poetic license with this one to give it more…flair." Or something.

"Nah, she's the real deal. It's so awesome," he muttered under his breath, then grinned.

It wasn't awesome, it was bizarre and Candace couldn't picture it. She was definitely calling her dad in the morning to get answers.

Just as they entered their suite, her phone rang. She dug it out of her purse and sighed when she saw Grandma's number on the display. "Dare I?" she asked Ryan.

"Hell, yes," he said, all excited as he reached for it. "Let me answer it."

Shooting him an annoyed frown, she angled her upper body away to block him and answered. "Hi."

"Hope I didn't interrupt anything?"

"Unfortunately no." Although she would have been if she'd called a minute later. "What's up?"

"Bring everybody back downstairs. I've called a meeting."

Her eyebrows rose. "Now? What for? It's midnight."

"Oh, you'll have lots of time to enjoy your young stud of a husband after. Come down and meet us in the study right away. It's important." The line went dead.

Exasperated, Candace growled and began punching in a text, beginning with the word *Sorry*. "Come on, we gotta go back downstairs. Grandma's apparently called us all to a meeting."

Ryan paused in the act of unbuttoning his shirt, his expression lighting up. "A secret meeting?"

"Who the hell knows?" She was definitely calling her dad to find out what was going on. Her grandma was a character, but sometimes Candace worried she was losing it. A little damage control or medical intervention might be in order here.

Ryan practically tore past her out into the hall, a giant grin on his face. "I can't wait to see what she's got up her sleeve."

Shaking her head, Candace finished typing out the message, then sent it to the others and followed Ryan back to the elevator. After receiving several WTF responses from the others, she replied that no, this wasn't a joke, and yes, there was in fact an actual meeting. She hoped.

On their way to the elevator a door opened behind them. Candace looked back to find Maya and Jackson hurrying after them. Maya was tying the sash on her robe tighter, her hair was mussed, and her lipstick was gone. Her blue-green eyes shot sparks at Candace as she strode toward them.

"This better be damn important, Ace." Jackson was right behind her, the laid-back Texan looking uncharacteristically annoyed. Yep, her text had definitely interrupted some sexy times.

"Yeah," she agreed, badly wanting some alone time with Ryan.

After their talk yesterday she was anxious to hash out the rest of what she wanted to say, as well as talk about the timing of having a family, and she also craved the intimate connection that came only from having him inside her. She wanted all of that tonight, so she hoped this meeting didn't last long. "It better."

By the time they reached the study, located off the lobby in the main building, the others were there waiting. Everyone was gathered around the rectangular table, along with a well-built, dark-haired man Candace didn't recognize. A scar ran along the side of his face and jaw, and his intense gray gaze and bearing told her immediately he had some kind of military or law enforcement training.

"Grandma," she said by way of greeting. "Okay, we're all here." *And nobody's too thrilled with you right now.* "What's this all about?"

Grandma stood and took her by the arm. "This is my granddaughter, Candace. The gunship pilot I told you about," she told the stranger proudly. "Candace, this is Declan MacKenzie."

She recognized the name. "Hello," she said, shaking hands with him. Everyone around these parts knew who the MacKenzies were. "MacKenzie, as in co-owner of this resort?"

The man's eyes warmed a fraction as he smiled. "Well, not just me. Mostly I run the family security company here out of Surrender with my brother, Shane."

"I understand you two know each other," Grandma said to Wade. "Being that you used to work for the same...organization."

So MacKenzie was a former spook? It made sense that he and Wade would have crossed paths, if he had in fact been with the CIA.

Wade inclined his head. "We know *of* each other. Good to meet you finally, MacKenzie."

"Likewise. That was great work on the Rahim case. One for the books."

"Yeah, it was memorable." Wade held out his hand.

The details of the Rahim case were classified, but the story had been splashed all over the news for weeks after the dirty bomb attack outside of CIA headquarters in Langley, Virginia. Erin had been directly caught up in it. Thankfully she had suffered only a broken arm and some mild radiation exposure, but Candace and their entire group knew all about what had happened.

Ryan wound an arm around her waist and she leaned into him, savoring the feel of his solid, muscular body against hers.

Wade shook hands with MacKenzie, then the man smiled at Erin. "And this must be your beautiful bride-to-be I've heard so much about."

She shook his hand. "I'm Erin. I'm a Montanan too, grew up outside of Billings. I recognize your name and know of your family."

"Well, sorry to interrupt your night, but given what Ruby told me tonight, I thought this needed to be looked into more."

"Sure, no problem." Erin took the seat Wade pulled out for her and scooted in closer to the table.

After all the introductions, Grandma clapped her hands once. "All right, let's sit down and get started."

"On what?"

She shot Candace an exasperated look. "On the camp your boys found up in the hills."

Everybody looked at MacKenzie.

"My company does contract work for the government. I've been gathering intel on something, and given what you found the other day, I thought you should all see what I've got."

They all moved closer to the table. A map was laid out in the center of it, this one complete with all the topographical information the previous one had lacked. "Ruby tells me the site you found was about here?" MacKenzie said to them.

Wade nodded. "Ryan's got the exact coordinates."

Ryan released her to pull them up again on his phone and MacKenzie marked them on the map. "And about how many casings would you say were out there?" the man asked.

"High hundreds at least, maybe more," Ryan said. "Some of the smaller trees up to about ten inches thick were cut in half by the volume of fire."

"Know something about it?" Cam asked, folding his arms across his chest.

"There've been rumors," MacKenzie said. "Stories about hunters hearing large volumes of fire in the distance, but no one's ever seen it happening. People are saying they've heard talk about a militia operating in the area."

Jackson frowned. "What kind of a militia?"

Wade spoke before MacKenzie could answer. "Are you talking about the March Madness?"

The man nodded, face grave. "Yes."

"What's that?" Candace asked, not liking the sound of it or the direction this was taking.

Wade straightened but kept his palms flat on the tabletop as he answered. "For over a year now there've been rumors of a guy named Eric March forming a secret militia here in Montana. He's former army, and after he was court-martialed and convicted of conduct unbecoming, he received a dishonorable discharge."

"What did he do?"

"Got caught up in the politics of war," Wade said. "Intervened to stop a nine-year-old boy from being raped by a villager and beat the shit out of the guy. Put him in the hospital. The villager pressed charges and the Afghan government put pressure on ours to do something. So to calm the situation down, they charged March with assault causing bodily harm, convicted him, and kicked him out of the army."

It disgusted Candace. "That's so twisted." He should have been praised for his actions, not punished.

"Yeah. Needless to say, he wasn't too happy, and now he's anti-government and looking to stir up shit by training his own militia to attack government installations across the state." His gaze shot to her grandma. "Sorry, Ruby." Apparently even Wade knew her grandma didn't like people cussing in front of her.

"No, something about this smells bad, so it's definitely shit," her grandma said. "He should have gotten a medal, not a conviction, but even though he was right to be angry, it doesn't excuse his current plans to arm and train people around here to attack the government. Does he pose a serious threat?"

Wade nodded. "Yep. And now word is, various agencies have been looking for him for a long time. He went off grid a few years back and no one's been able to find a trace of him since. Unless we did just that last night," he added, looking at the other guys.

"Got a file on him here," MacKenzie said, laying a manila folder on the table and opening it to reveal a picture of March.

Candace studied it. White male, early forties. Graying, light brown hair, blue eyes.

"Latest intel estimates his followers are numbered around a thousand or so, but it could be more. His ability to avoid detection and capture says a lot about his capabilities. Wherever he is, he's well stocked and has had lots of time to plan whatever he has in mind."

"Potential domestic terrorist attacks?" Maya asked him.

"Yes."

Candace glanced at MacKenzie, putting it all together. "And so you think maybe the site the guys found yesterday is possibly where this militia trains? Or that maybe March is using the old bunker systems?"

"We were told they were all destroyed at the end of the Cold War," her grandma said, her gaze sliding from MacKenzie to Wade.

"You ever go back there, after it was destroyed?" Wade asked.

"No," she admitted, looking pensive.

"Ruby, where did you say the entrance to the bunker system is?" MacKenzie asked.

"Somewhere around here," she said, circling an area on the map with her fingertip. "Not too far from that rock formation I told you about earlier."

"When's the last time you were down there?"

"Right after the fall of the Berlin wall. We went there to help clean it out before they destroyed the complex."

"They didn't destroy it," Wade said, face grim. "At least not the entire thing."

Struggling to take all this in, Candace gaped at her grandmother. "Does my dad know any of this?"

"Course he does. He's a senator."

"Then why the hell am I just finding out about this for the first time today? I've still got my security clearance."

Her grandma shrugged. "Never seemed important enough to mention before, and you never asked."

Candace gave Ryan a disbelieving look. "Unreal."

"What are the chances that anyone saw you?" MacKenzie said, and the guys all got quiet.

Too quiet.

Ryan shook his head. "We split up and searched the immediate area before setting up camp. There was no one else out there."

"You're sure?"

Ryan hesitated a moment, and Candace's heart sank. He glanced at Wade, then Jackson and Cam. "Not a hundred percent, no. It's possible he had cameras or some other kind of surveillance equipment set up that we didn't find."

So then a domestic terrorist might have seen them looking in the area. She reached for Ryan's hand, dread squeezing her stomach. He twined his fingers through hers, gripped in reassurance but it didn't make her feel any warmer.

"You gonna check it out?" Ryan asked MacKenzie, releasing her hand to wind an arm around her shoulders and tug her close. She wrapped her arms around his waist and leaned her cheek on his chest, told herself there was no reason for her to worry.

He nodded. "I'll call it into my local FBI contact and do some recon. At the very least we'll want to search the area and check out the site and the bunkers."

"No need." Maya pulled out her phone and stood. "I'll call my boss right now. He'll spread the word, get the right people in touch with you. They can have a team out here by morning."

MacKenzie gave her a nod. "Appreciate that." He glanced at the rest of them. "You're all here for another few days, if we need more for the investigation?"

"Until Sunday," Ryan said, running his fingers through the ends of her hair, the soothing motion doing nothing to stem her growing anxiety.

MacKenzie closed the file and stood. "Thanks for coming down. I'll be in touch when I have an update. You all have a good night."

As he left, Candace looked up questioningly at Ryan. He gave her a gentle smile and cupped the side of her face in his free hand. "Don't worry, it's fine. Nothing's gonna happen."

It better not. They'd been through so much together already. He was her beating heart, her whole world. Which was why she felt it so keenly when he hurt her.

Ryan kept his arm solidly wrapped around her shoulders as they walked back to their room together, but she couldn't shake the worry that had taken root inside her. There was nothing she could do about that situation, however, so she let it go and focused on something she could control—finishing the talk she and Ryan had started yesterday morning.

So much of their future hinged on resolving her career issue, and she wanted his support in whatever direction she took next. She wanted to know they were on the same page with everything, and make plans for the future.

The moment they got back to their room, she was laying it all on the line.

* * * *

"We've got a problem," Lyle said through the phone.

At the grave tone, Eric braced himself for bad news. His second-in-command had been working with a few others all day to find out more information about their unwanted guests from last night, and clean up what they'd left behind at the training site. "Not my favorite words to hear, but all right then. What have you got?"

"I got IDs on all four of them, from someone working the front desk at the resort. We're still looking into two of them but I already got a hit on the others when I did a search and ran them past my contact, and it's not good news. Staff Sergeant Ryan Wentworth and Tech Sergeant Cam Munro are both AFSOC."

Shit. "And the other two are military as well?"

"Not sure yet, but the front desk clerk said they're supposedly all here for a wedding that's scheduled for Saturday morning. What do you think?"

"I think it's possible, but it still seems like one hell of a coincidence that they show up here snooping around right as we're getting to the end stages of planning the first operation. And I'd bet my favorite assault rifle that the other two guys are either military or even SOF-trained as well. You saw the way they moved." Just like he and his men used to back in Afghanistan.

Lyle pushed out a long breath. "Yeah."

Eric dragged a hand over his face, his mind whirling. "They've seen too much. There's no way they found all those casings, the tracks, and the shredded trees and didn't report it to someone." He shook his head. "We can't risk leaving things the way they are. This has to be dealt with. Tonight."

"All right." Lyle didn't sound too happy about it and Eric wasn't either. This was a risk none of them could afford, but he had to be proactive. "What are you thinking?"

"Some kind of a diversion at the resort. Something small-scale that looks either like an accident or a case of mistaken identity. We have to divert attention away from us and the site so we can evacuate the area." And he also wanted to make a statement. Let the government know he was a force to be reckoned with, hit at least one target before he went on the run. Those men who had found the training site would serve his purposes nicely.

Changing locations now, at this critical hour, was a huge goddamn headache and inconvenience he couldn't afford. It would take days for them to pull it off completely, but he needed a solid window of at least a few hours to dismantle the most critical equipment and get it to a safe house where he could hide.

Because cops and Feds would be out hunting him now, and it meant all his work and the painstaking precautions he'd taken in setting up headquarters here were finished. He was looking at months of disruption, of being on the run and changing safe houses every day to stay one step ahead of the authorities that had been hunting for him for the past three years. He had no choice.

"I'll call up some of the guys," Lyle said.

"No. I want just you and our three best soldiers." He typed in some commands on his laptop and pulled up his personnel files.

After scanning the reports and spreadsheets he kept on each member, he named the three men he wanted for this op. The best marksmen with the most trustworthy backgrounds. "Call them now and alert them to be on standby. Then I want you in here immediately so we can plan everything together. Once we know what the diversion will be, you'll meet up with the others and outfit them at a staging area." One well away from this site.

"Got it."

He checked the time. "I want this planned and the boys ready to go by oh-two-hundred hours." The timing was critical. He had to be out of here and in the clear before the Feds or whoever else arrived.

"Understood. I'll be there shortly."

Eric disconnected and checked all his security cameras surrounding the entrance to the bunker system, and farther out around the inner perimeter. Nothing moved in the view of the infrared cameras and no alarms had been tripped, but the uneasy feeling in the pit of his stomach was growing stronger by the minute.

He was out of time and everything hinged on him getting this place sanitized before he left it. The best defense was a good offense, so he was going to strike before anyone could come after him.

Chapter Eight

By the time they made it back to their room a few minutes later, it was almost one in the morning. Candace headed straight for the bathroom to brush her teeth and get ready for bed, unable to shake the anxiety that had followed her from the meeting.

Though judging from the way Ryan had just pinned her to the elevator wall on the way up a few moments ago, it was clear he wasn't even thinking about a possible threat and was raring to have sex the moment she stepped out into the bedroom. On the one hand she wanted more of that connection with her husband, but on the other, she was too caught up in her head to be able to enjoy it right now.

She smoothed her hands down the front of her dress, suddenly nervous about what she had to say. Well, more about his reaction and response to it. But putting it off any longer wasn't an option.

When she stepped out of the bathroom a few minutes later, however, she wavered. Ryan was stretched out on the bed watching her, stark naked, one muscular arm tucked beneath his head. Pure, decadent sin.

"Come over here," he said in that low, sexy voice that always made her insides clench in anticipation.

She faltered for a moment, drinking in the sight of that beautiful, hard male body waiting for her. *You can still enjoy him afterward, Candace.*

She raised her eyes to his, cleared her throat. "I want to talk."

His face went blank, then wariness crept into his eyes. "Now?"

"Yes, now." She'd never be able to sleep tonight until this was cleared up.

"Can't we talk after?"

He was such a guy. "Sex doesn't solve everything, Ryan," she said, frustration making her voice sharper than she'd intended.

A slight frown creased his forehead as he slowly sat up and propped himself against the headboard. "Okay... Is this about what MacKenzie said?"

"No. Well, partly." Letting out a deep breath, she crossed to the bed and sat on it, her hip inches from his. She'd thought about how to word this for weeks now, had to make it clear so he understood. "I miss you."

He searched her eyes for a long moment, as though she were a puzzle he was trying to figure out. "I'm right here."

She lifted a hand to stroke his face, let her fingers linger on the soft whiskers of his beard. She'd been bottling this up for so long and now she had to let it out. "I told you most of it yesterday, but there's more." When he waited, she continued. "I feel like we're drifting apart and I'm scared if we don't stop it, that it might lead to big problems between us. Like, us turning into near strangers and our marriage falling apart."

At that he sat up straighter, concern on his face. "Why would you think that?"

Was she really the only one who felt this way? She wasn't crazy; they *had* been drifting apart. How could he not have felt it, or at least noticed? She twisted her fingers together in her lap. "We just...we're not as close as we used to be. Emotionally."

He slipped an arm around her hips and dragged her onto his lap to tuck her into the cradle of his body. The ache in her heart eased the moment his arms closed around her. Heavy and strong. Loving. "I know we've been apart a lot over the past couple years, but that hasn't changed the way I feel about you one bit. I love you even more now than I did the day I married you."

She lifted her head to look into his mahogany-brown eyes. "You do?"

"Of course," he said, sounding offended that she'd question it. "Why, are you saying you don't love me the way you used to?"

"I do; I just feel like we're not as close as we were and I miss that. And I'm not trying to make you feel guilty about being away— you know I'm well aware of what your job requires and that I fully support your career. But I miss us. I miss my husband," she finished, her stupid voice catching as her throat locked up. She didn't even know if she was making sense, but she didn't know how else to word it. "I miss being in bed with you and waking up with you there, being able to talk to you about anything and everything. Making plans together for our life."

He stiffened slightly. "I tried to stay in touch with you this last time as much as I could."

"I know, but in all our e-mails and phone calls, we mostly talked about surface stuff, especially after that tense call. Nothing really important about what we want, or anything about our future as a couple."

"So you're saying...what? You want me to quit?"

"No," she said, aghast that he'd even think she'd ask that of him. "I know how much you love your job, and if you quit because of me you'd resent me for it."

He visibly relaxed. "What then?"

"I guess I want us both to try harder when we're apart," she said, tracing her fingertips over the notch between his collarbones. "We both need to make more of an effort to stay connected with one another on an emotional level."

She was quiet a moment. "Remember when we were out in those mountains together? It was the scariest thing I've ever been through, not gonna lie, but I'd never felt closer to anyone than I did to you then. And for those few weeks afterward as well."

"If you're saying you want us to get trapped behind enemy lines together in the Hindu Kush during the dead of winter so we can bond again, I'm gonna have to pass," he said dryly.

She couldn't help but laugh, beginning to feel stupid and insecure and wishing she hadn't brought this up. "No, I wouldn't ever want to go through something like that again either. My point was, I miss the strength of the link we had then. And I still really want to have a family. Sooner rather than later. I'm willing to be a single stay-at-home mom for a little while, but I don't want to raise our kids all by myself while you're overseas all the time. We need to plan for that together."

He nodded. "That's fair, I get it. And if we had kids, I wouldn't want to not be there for them either."

She tipped her head back. "When do you want to start a family?"

"In a couple more years maybe. Definitely before you hit thirty-five; otherwise your eggs might all be dried up."

She poked him in the chest, smirking at his dry humor. "My eggs are just fine, thanks very much. You just worry about your swimmers."

"You mean my fast-movers."

"Sure, your fast-movers then," she said, smiling at the reminder of what he'd said to Cam yesterday morning. Laying her head against his sturdy shoulder, she snuggled deeper into his embrace, already feeling ten times closer to him than she had in a long time. "And what about my job?"

He stroked a hand over her hair. "If you really want to get out that badly, then you should get out."

The words sent a wave of relief washing over her. "What if I can't find anything I want to do once I get out?"

"Then we'll handle it when the time comes. Clamp down a little tighter with the finances until you do find something."

She wound her arms around him, tightened them, a sense of peace blanketing her. "Thank you."

"Welcome. We good now?"

The hopeful note in his voice, along with the hot gleam in his eyes when she glanced up at him, made her smile. *Such* a guy, wanting to get straight to the make-up sex portion of the evening. "Yes. We're good."

"Great. Now come here." He scooped her up and turned her, the muscles in his shoulders and chest bunching as he reached up to take her face between his hands. "I love you more than anything, and I missed you like hell while I was gone."

Relief poured through her. He wasn't very romantic, or flowery with his words, so his saying that to her now meant the world to her.

"I missed you more." And for the first time in months, she felt like they were finally in sync again. A huge relief.

Now she wanted the special intimacy that only their physical connection could bring.

Bracing her hands on his broad shoulders, she bent and covered his lips with hers. He nipped at her lower lip, ran his tongue across it then sucked gently, his hands framing her face, taking complete control.

She sighed and made a soft purring sound as she opened for him, hungry for more of the heat he'd ignited in her. Just as things were starting to get interesting, she jolted when the fire alarm blared to life.

Ryan stilled and lifted his head, instantly on alert.

Coming up on her knees, she looked up at the ceiling and inhaled deeply. There was no smoke and the air seemed clean. "Smell anything?"

"No." He rolled out from under her and peeked out the window. "Don't see anything."

"Must be a false alarm. Come back here." She grabbed his shoulder and turned him back toward her.

Grinning, he resumed his former position beneath her and cupped his hands around her breasts, his thumbs brushing over the hard, sensitive tips. "My sexy wife." He kissed the side of her neck, the brush of his beard making her tingle all over despite the continued blare of the fire alarm. "Just ignore it and focus on me." He turned her face back to his, slanted his mouth across hers before skimming his way over her jaw, to her throat.

"Mmm…" She tipped her head back to give him more room, running her hands over his bare back. The sheer power of him never failed to get her hot. Then Ryan rolled her over onto her back and blanketed her with his weight, the hard ridge of his erection pressing against her throbbing mound.

She sighed and threaded her fingers into his hair, letting her eyes drift close, the sound of the fire alarm fading beneath the rush of desire.

Something flickered against her closed eyelids.

Her body went rigid as she opened her eyes and saw the yellow-orange glow flickering through the window. "Ryan." She pushed at his shoulder.

At the urgency in her voice he sat up and reached for the blind covering the window, shoving it aside to look down. A second later, she smelled it. Faint, but unmistakable.

Smoke.

Ryan jumped off the bed and pulled on his underwear. "Something's burning down there," he said, reaching for his jeans. "Get dressed."

* * * *

After yanking on his boots, Ryan unlocked their door and opened it to check the hallway. The moment he did the scent of smoke grew stronger, and there was a faint haze in the air. Maya and Jackson's door opened and Jackson stuck his head out.

"Not a false alarm," Ryan told him. "Meet you guys outside?"

"Yeah." Jackson slammed the door shut behind him.

Ryan ducked back inside and turned to Candace, who was pulling on a sweater. "We should go."

Calm but decisive, his wife hurried to the dresser across the room to grab some things. "I'll get our IDs and wallets. You get the weapons."

Good call. Leaving live ammo in a fire wasn't an awesome idea. He went to the closet, grabbed his jacket, and then the hunting gear Wade had loaned him.

Candace was pulling on her shoes when he met her at the door. "Any idea where it is or how far it's spread?" she asked.

"Definitely on the ground floor at our end of the building. Not sure how big it is yet." Just as he said it the emergency sprinkler system activated overhead, spraying them with cold water. "Come on," he said, pulling open the door, rifle in hand and the rest of his gear in the backpack slung over his shoulder.

She stepped into the hallway and turned right, toward the far end of the hall opposite where the flames were, where that stairwell would hopefully be clear. Maya and Jackson appeared behind them a few moments later. There were only four rooms per floor, and no one answered when Ryan pounded on the others, so there was no one else to warn and clear out.

The smoke grew thicker every second, the blare of the fire alarm echoing off the walls and ceiling. He moved in front of Candace as they neared the far stairwell door and opened it to check that it was safe. The lights were still on inside and the air was clearer here.

"Clear." Ryan took the lead, with Candace behind him, then Maya and Jackson bringing up the rear. They were almost to the third floor when the stairwell door there shoved open to reveal Wade, Erin, Cam, and Dev. "This is sure an exciting wedding trip you two've got going on here so far," he said to Wade.

Wade grunted and held the door for the others while holding his rifle, his own gear packed into a duffel in his free hand. "I was hoping for a lot less excitement, believe me."

"Yeah, us too," Devon muttered as she entered the stairwell, the soles of her running shoes slapping against the concrete steps.

Together they headed for the second floor, slowing to allow other guests ahead of them to file down the concrete steps and toward the exit on the first floor. An elderly couple wearing the resort's robes and slippers were the first to leave the building, then a younger couple with their small daughter, followed by a middle-aged woman and her poodle.

When it was finally their turn, Ryan neared the door and glimpsed the flames at the opposite end of the building. They were already halfway up the front of it and climbing toward their room.

"We're good." He held the door open that led to the flagstone patio outside, watching the flames licking at the wooden exterior while Candace and the others filed past him into the open.

The moment he released the door and stepped outside, the unmistakable crack of a rifle filled the air. He froze, automatically scanning to see where it had come from.

More cracks rang out, and a bullet smashed into the front of the building two yards away from him.

Shit.

People screamed and scattered in different directions. Reacting on pure instinct, Ryan gripped his rifle and immediately turned for his wife.

Candace was already running for cover but he caught her around the ribs and took her to the ground, shielding her with his larger body, one hand wrapped around the back of her head to protect her skull from the impact.

As they hit the hard surface of the stone patio, a hot, burning pain lanced through his right upper arm and tore across his ribs.

Chapter Nine

You gotta be fucking kidding *me.*

Ryan bit back a growl of rage and pain as he rolled off Candace and grabbed her arm to drag her behind cover, his right hand slick already with blood as he clutched the rifle.

She scrambled up onto her hands and knees, crawling beside him while blood ran down the length of his right arm. He'd served a total of six combat tours in Iraq and Afghanistan, managed to avoid any bullet holes throughout all of them, but he wound up getting shot at a fucking resort in *Montana*?

So wrong.

People were still screaming and running all over the place. Someone was still out there shooting at them.

Ignoring the pain, focused on getting them to safety, he shoved to his hands and knees, dragged Candace up, and took off in a running crouch, her hand clutched tightly in his left one. Bullets slammed into the rock wall a few feet beside him, sending up a spray of razor-sharp shards.

"Go, go," he urged her, flinging her in front of him toward safety.

Two strides from the corner of the building ahead of them, another shot splintered the air. Candace flinched and clapped a hand to her side an instant before she disappeared from view.

His heart shot into his throat. He dove around the corner just as more bullets punched into the fieldstone wall behind him where he had been only a split second before.

The instant he hit the ground, a hand grabbed him and hauled him the rest of the way behind cover. He rolled over to find Cam bending over him.

"You hit?" the PJ yelled over the chaotic noise and confusion around them.

Ryan didn't answer, his only concern finding his wife. Turning onto his left side, he pushed up and scanned frantically for her.

She was crouched down against the stone foundation of the building, her face pale, a stream of blood trickling through her fingers as she pressed a hand to her upper left side and his anger evaporated as raw fear punched through him. *"Candace."*

Her dark gaze met his, wide and startled. "I'm okay," she blurted.

No, she wasn't. He was already rolling to his feet, rushing for her. "She's hit."

"So are you," Cam said, clamping a hand on his good shoulder and shoving him back down. "Stay the hell put so I can take a look."

He wrenched away and opened his mouth to tell his buddy to fuck off, but Erin was already crawling her way to Candace. "I've got her." She took Candace by the shoulders, saying something he couldn't hear. Fuck, how bad was she hit?

Ryan shoved Cam away and rolled to his feet. His wife was fucking bleeding; he didn't care about himself.

Cam let him go but followed close behind. Whoever was out there shooting was quiet now, but that didn't mean the threat was over. Ryan crouched next to Candace, set a hand on her shoulder and cupped the side of her face with the other, the burn of his wound barely registering beneath his alarm. Her dark brown eyes were dazed, glazed with pain. "Baby..."

"No, I'm fine," she insisted, the words choppy, her breath coming in gasps. "I'm breathing okay and I can move my arm. I don't think it hit anything serious. What about you?" She ran her free hand down his right arm.

"I'm good." The bullet hole stung like someone had poured fucking battery acid into it, but he could still move his arm so he figured it wasn't broken, even if parts of it had gone numb and some of his muscles were weak.

He rubbed her back with his left hand, feeling helpless. God, if he'd even for one moment thought there might be a threat waiting for them outside, he never would have exited the building like that.

Erin already had Candace's sweater up and was examining the wound just under the edge of her shoulder blade. She'd worked at Craig Joint Theater Hospital at Bagram for multiple tours, and had seen every kind of trauma case imaginable. "It's still in there, buried under the edge of her scapula. Must have been a ricochet." She looked up into Candace's face. "Do your ribs hurt when you breathe?"

She shook her head. "Not really."

Erin nodded. "Anywhere else hurt? Your shoulder blade?"

"I said I'm fine." She thrust out her right hand toward him. "Now give me a damn weapon so I can shoot back at these assholes."

Ryan slipped a hand around her nape and leaned in to plant a hard kiss on her mouth. "You got it."

Erin glanced at him. "She'll be okay. I'll try to dig the bullet out and get the bleeding stopped as best I can until we can get clear."

Ryan nodded, shrugged off his pack, and dug out his pistol. After slamming in a fresh magazine, he handed it to Candace. If the shooters maintained their distance, it wouldn't do her much good, but at least she'd feel better being armed.

Now that he wasn't frozen with terror that his wife was going to die, he scanned the others, all hidden behind this low retaining wall running the length of this side of the building.

Wade was on his phone, probably talking to the cops, rifle in his free hand. Ryan grabbed ammo from his pack and loaded his rifle. His right upper arm and the back of his hand were numb, the bullet wound burning like fire.

Rolling to his belly, he crawled his way over to where Jackson lay near the end of the protective wall with his own weapon trained toward the shooters. Maya was right next to him with her service pistol, searching for a target.

As he neared them, the back of Ryan's neck prickled. All eight of them were now pinned down behind this low rock wall with an unknown number of shooters out there, making them one giant, fat target.

They couldn't stay here. He and everyone else with a rifle had to lay down covering fire while the others spread out and found a better defensive position.

Ryan bit back a grunt of pain as he nestled the stock of his weapon against his right shoulder, pressing his right cheek to it to stare through the scope. The night vision device would enable him to see a potential target in the darkness, but it wasn't as good as having NVGs.

"See any muzzle flashes?" he asked the others, aware of the blood that continued to run down his arm, puddling on the flagstone beneath his bent elbow.

"A couple at one o'clock a few seconds ago," Maya answered. Then to Jackson, "I hit one, but I don't think he's down. Got anything?"

"Not yet," he answered, his Texas drawl making his voice seem even calmer.

Wade made his way over to crouch on one knee beside them. "How we looking?"

"No targets yet," Ryan answered. Who the hell had opened fire on them?

"Cops are on the way and I just got off a call with MacKenzie. He's alerting the local Feds and is on his way here with his brother. Said he's bringing backup."

Well, until then, they were on their own. "We gotta get the hell out from behind this wall," Ryan muttered. Who knew how many shooters there were, and what kind of weapons they had? It made his skin crawl to stay here another second.

"Yeah," Wade muttered, putting his eye to his scope.

Quickly they came up with a plan. Candace still held the pistol tight in her right hand, her expression intent as Erin did what she could to stop the bleeding.

Ryan wanted to haul her into his arms and not let go but he couldn't until this threat was neutralized. He loved his wife so damn much, respected how strong and brave she was. He couldn't stand to lose her, wanted to have a family with her someday. She was *everything* to him.

"You and Erin get to cover while we divert them," he said to her. "Maya and Dev, you'll cover them while we head out."

Both women nodded once, gazes trained on the darkness beyond. "Got it," Maya answered.

"Ready?" he asked the guys. They all nodded.

On his three count, Ryan and Wade burst out from behind the wall, firing spaced shots across the patio toward where the shooting had come from. Cam, Jackson, and Maya laid down covering fire for them as he and Wade sprinted to the relative protection of the water feature on the opposite side.

Flashes of light burst in the darkness and rounds slammed into the rocks in front of them. Bleeding and royally pissed off by this point, Ryan ducked around the corner of the fountain and caught sight of one of the shooters in his scope. He aimed and fired two shots, hitting him center mass. The guy cried out and fell.

"One shooter down," he said to Wade, wishing he had comms with the others so they knew what was going on.

"I saw two more moving northeast."

Swiveling around, Ryan waved to signal the others and Jackson signaled back. They were ready. He faced forward again, searching through his scope for another target. He and Wade began firing again, laying down covering fire so the rest of their group could move.

"We're clear," Cam called out a minute later.

Ryan's heart rate eased and when he looked back there was no one left behind the wall. Candace was now out of sight behind solid cover with Erin to treat her wound, and Dev and Maya were both armed as well. She was in good hands, and as safe as he could make her for the moment.

Now he and the guys had to hunt down the rest of these bastards before anyone else got hurt.

He signaled to Cam and Jackson, hiding behind the end of a short brick wall that separated the patio from the garden, then resumed firing to keep the shooters at bay and give the PJs time to join him and Wade.

Thirty seconds later, Cam and Jackson reached them, rifles to their shoulders and ready to rock.

"Two more shooters moving to the northeast," he told them. "We'll go in pairs. Wade and I'll take the right, you two take the left."

"Roger that," Jackson murmured, eye to his scope.

He and Wade peeled off and started across the north lawn while Cam and Jackson covered them. They stopped behind a decorative rock formation in the middle of the grass and covered the other guys, then kept leapfrogging their way toward where the shooters had been.

The one Ryan had hit was gone, but there was a blood trail for them to follow, though it was hard to see with just his scope to aid them in the darkness.

Either the shooter was still mobile or someone else was dragging him. No matter what, he couldn't have gone far.

Ducking around the tree he was hiding behind, Ryan jerked back when a bullet struck the trunk, sending up a hail of splinters.

Wade immediately fired from Ryan's left. "Got him."

Good. Two down. "See anyone else?"

"Nope."

"Anything?" he called out to Cam and Jackson.

"Negative," Cam answered.

There could be more than two remaining shooters out here, but if they were lucky, maybe not.

Then, in the distance, came the sound of an engine roaring to life. He eased around the tree trunk and scanned the terrain with his scope. A flash of movement caught his attention.

Zeroing in on it, he saw someone driving away on an ATV. "One target on an ATV moving northwest. Can't get a clear shot through the trees."

"I see him," Wade muttered. "No shot though."

And it wasn't like they could catch up to him on foot either. Dammit.

"Contact, ten o'clock," Jackson said to their left.

Ryan swung the barrel of his weapon toward the new target and caught sight of a man running between the trees. He was cradling his arm, seemed to be struggling. "I got him. Cover me."

Stepping out from behind the relative protection of the tree, he rushed forward. Behind him he could hear Wade following. On silent feet he moved over the short-cut grass and into the trees, knowing the others had his back.

He lost sight of the target for a moment, then the wounded man burst out from behind a stand of trees. He stumbled, went down on one knee, and it was the break Ryan needed.

Ryan raced straight at him. "Drop your weapon and put your fucking hands up!"

The man grabbed his weapon and whipped around, trying to raise it in time to get a shot off.

Ryan's hands were rock steady, the pain barely noticeable now as he aimed the barrel of his rifle at the target and fired.

The man shouted and dropped to his back, his weapon lying on the ground. Ryan's boots pounded over the carpet of fallen leaves as he ran for the man. When he reached the man he kicked the fallen rifle away, aiming his own at the guy at point blank range.

The shooter had half turned onto his side, his breathing ragged and uneven. "Don't...don't kill me," he rasped out, grimacing as he struggled to bring his hands up.

Wade moved in like a deadly shadow to search him for weapons, then grabbed the guy by the front of his camo fatigues and shook him once. "Who the fuck are you and why did you attack us?" he growled.

"Or...orders," the man said, voice weak.

Ryan wasn't exactly sure where he'd hit the guy, but from the raspy breathing it sounded like he'd gotten the guy in the lung. If they didn't get what they needed to know out of him now, they probably weren't going to. "Whose orders?" he demanded.

"Boss..."

Wade let him drop back to the ground with a dull thud and leaned over him. "March?"

Something flared in the man's eyes at the mention of the name, then he closed them. "Orders..."

Wade shot Ryan a hard look and pushed to his feet.

"You get him?" Cam's voice called out.

"Yeah, we're good. Any other targets?"

"Just the one on the ATV."

Ryan stared down at the nearly unconscious man. "Let's get him back to the resort. If we can stabilize him, the cops might be able to get more information out of him."

"I got him." Wade handed Ryan his weapon and bent to hoist the wounded man over his shoulders.

"Let's get back," Ryan said, anxious to get back to Candace and report what they'd found.

When he rushed into the resort's main building and through the lobby to the lounge ten minutes later, all sweaty from the run and a little chilled from blood loss, he found all the guests huddled together there. Maya and Devon were standing guard with two male resort employees. Where was Candace?

His heart squeezed when he spotted her off to one side of the room with her grandma, still wearing that blood-stained T-shirt, his pistol in her hand. A staggering wave of relief hit him, then she gave a little smile and started toward him.

He met her halfway and caught her around the back in a tight, one-armed hug, careful not to touch her wound and totally ignoring her grandma, hovering at her side. "Sweetheart, you okay?" He buried his sweaty face in her hair, breathing her in. She was safe. That was all that mattered.

She nodded and hugged him with her right arm, pressing frantic kisses against his throat and jaw. "Yes, but you're bleeding pretty bad."

"I'll take care of that," Jackson said, coming up beside him with a first aid kit. "Hold still and let me at least patch you up for the time being."

Ryan stood still and let Jackson do his thing, biting back a wince as he probed at the wound. "Did it go through?"

"Yeah. Right through your tricep and then along your side for a few inches."

That would explain why his arm and the spot just under it burned so bad, from all the torn-up tissue.

Candace dragged her gaze from the wound and up to his face, her expression pinched with worry. "You're not okay."

He kissed the bridge of her nose, her mouth. "I'm good. More worried about you."

She shook her head. "I was lucky, Erin says it only hit skin and muscle. She managed to dig out the bullet, give me a few stitches, and bandage me up. I'm not even bleeding anymore, just sore." She reached for his left hand, her cold fingers wrapping around it tight. "Can you still use your arm?"

"Yeah, it's fine." He didn't tell her about the numbness or loss of grip strength because there were more important things to worry about at the moment. "Love you."

"Love you too." She cupped the side of his face in her hand. "Did you get them?"

"We got three of the shooters, but the fourth got away on an ATV."

Wade waved them over, tucking his cell phone back into his pocket. "MacKenzie's almost here, and apparently he's got a big lead. We're supposed to meet him on the front lawn in two minutes." He glanced at Jackson as the PJ shoved something into the wound.

Ryan sucked in a breath and gritted his teeth, his vision wavering for a second at the swift, sudden burn.

Wade frowned at him. "You still good to go?"

"Yes," he said between his teeth.

Leaving the rest of the guests behind with the resort security, who were scrambling to secure the scene, Ryan took Candace's hand and walked with the others to the front entrance and out onto the lawn where the resort security had set up a perimeter. He didn't want to let her out of his sight even for a moment. Cops and fire trucks were just showing up on scene.

Then a familiar pulse overhead broke the silence. All of them stopped and looked skyward.

"I'd know that sound anywhere," Devon said, craning her neck to search for the approaching helo.

Yeah, they all would.

Moments later the unmistakable outline of a Blackhawk appeared overhead. It circled the wide north lawn once, then touched down in the center of it and two men hopped out. Declan MacKenzie and someone Ryan didn't recognize.

They jogged over, in full tac gear. "Satellite feed just showed the fourth shooter heading by ATV in the direction of the location you guys found in the mountains," MacKenzie said to them over the noise of the rotors. "Intel says it could be Eric March's second-in-command."

"You think he's headed for the bunkers?" Ryan asked, aware of the way Candace had tensed beside him. He stroked his thumb over the back of her hand in reassurance.

"Maybe, and if we're lucky, March will still be in the area. This is my brother, Shane, by the way. Former SEAL, now works ops with me," he said, motioning to the black-haired, dark-eyed man next to him, who nodded at them. "I've talked with my FBI contacts. There's no way they can get a team here in the next hour. So they've given us the green light to go after March and his men before they can make it out of the area. You guys up for a night mission?"

Fuck yes. "You got gear for us?" Ryan asked, releasing Candace's hand to wrap his left arm around her shoulders and pull her into him.

"On the bird."

Perfect.

"Wait a second, what about us?"

Ryan and MacKenzie both glanced at Maya, who was staring at them with a furious expression. Candace was glaring at them too.

Maya raised a dark eyebrow at them, her stare burning holes through them all before narrowing on MacKenzie. "You need operators, then I'm in."

MacKenzie watched her a moment, then nodded. "I've got gear on board for four. You guys need to figure out in a hurry who's coming."

Ryan whirled to face Candace. "You're not going," he told her flatly before she could say anything. "You need to stay here and talk to the cops, and help guard the other guests—"

"But—"

"*No.*" There was no fucking way he was allowing her to come. It had nothing to do with not trusting her ability, and everything to do with wanting her safe. She was wounded and in pain, and he just couldn't deal with the thought of putting her through anything else. He wrapped his left hand around her nape, squeezed as he stared into her eyes. "I need to know you're back here, safe."

"I—"

He cut her off by sliding his left hand into her hair and bringing his mouth down over hers in a hot, hard kiss before raising his head. "Please," he murmured.

She relented, but she didn't look happy about it, and her eyes were troubled. "You better not come back with any more holes in you," she muttered.

His wife rocked. "I won't."

Maya came over and wound an arm around Candace's waist. "If there's only enough equipment for you guys, then I guess I'll stay and help get the place locked down, keep my eye on her with Dev and Erin."

Ryan nodded once. "Thanks." He kissed Candace once more and left her with her friends, relieved that she was in good hands. Any one of those women would protect her with their life.

"So you know where the bunker location is then?" Wade asked MacKenzie as Ryan and the other guys headed for the bird together.

"Not exactly, but March's 2IC will. And just in case he doesn't go quietly and tell us what we want to know, we'll take along a little insurance." His gaze swept past them to Candace's grandma, standing with the other women. "Ruby," he called out. "You game for a little recon mission?"

Her eyes lit up like she'd just been offered a private tour of a rye distillery. "I was born ready, young man. Someone help me onto that chopper." With that she swept past the other women and headed for the waiting helo.

Chapter Ten

Wait, *what?*

Candace lunged forward and snagged her grandma's arm before she could take another step. For a woman her age, Ruby was in damn good shape, but her arm felt frail and delicate in Candace's grip. Her grandmother had no business going on that helo. "No way."

The guys stopped and looked back at them, and Grandma hiked her eyebrows up to her hairline. "*Excuse* me?"

"You can't go with them; it's insane." Candace tugged her back toward the resort entrance, determined to drag her there if necessary.

No surprise, Grandma dug in her heels. Literally. "Don't you dare tell me what I can and cannot do, young lady," she snapped, indignation stamped all over her wrinkled face as she wrenched her arm free.

Fighting back the urge to yell at her, Candace sucked in a deep breath and prayed for patience. "It's too dangerous. You have no training." At least nothing current.

Her chin lifted, pale green eyes glittering. "I have enough training for this. For God's sake, it's not like I'm going to be storming the bunkers with them." Her face brightened with excitement and she glanced back at the men. "Will I be storming the bunker with you?"

"*No,*" Ryan and MacKenzie immediately answered in unison.

Grandma's face fell a little as she switched her focus back to Candace. "There. See? I'm just going for a little ride, and maybe a night hike to find the entrance if they need me to."

Dammit… "Then I'm coming too."

The instant she said it, a bolt of uncontrollable, visceral fear sliced through her. Without warning, images of that hellish mission gone wrong in eastern Afghanistan flashed through her head like a high-speed slide show.

Her heart seized, then shot into a sickening gallop, turning her hands cold and clammy. It was like she was right back there again, trapped in those mountains while a blizzard raged and the enemy hunted them.

Everything inside her froze, her lungs, her blood. Her crewman's face was so vivid in her mind. Dover stared up at her from the edge of the cliff he dangled from, the sheer terror in his eyes sending a shudder through her now. He'd been trying to help her up the mountain when he'd slipped.

She'd watched, helpless, unable to do a damn thing for him. A moment later he'd lost his grip and fallen, his chilling screams scraping over her psyche. The sound of his body hitting the rocks was something she'd never be rid of. No amount of time or therapy could ever erase something like that.

She'd sat with him in the cave after they'd retrieved his body, sat by uselessly as he'd slipped away. Had zipped the body bag closed over his face, knowing he'd never see his wife and child again.

Ryan had been there with her. He'd been her rock, her anchor and safe haven. Losing him would kill her. It terrified her to think of the dangers he would face when he climbed out of that helo tonight.

Shaking off the harrowing thoughts, she forced herself back to the present, then clamped her hand around her grandma's forearm and started toward the guys. She did not *want* to get on that helo. The very thought of doing so made her skin crawl and her stomach pitch.

But she would go along if it meant protecting her grandmother and helping Ryan.

She started for the Blackhawk.

More heel digging. Grandma struggled and pulled them to a stop, twisting her arm free. "Don't be ridiculous! You're wounded, and I need you here to take care of the guests. You were a Bradford longer than you've been a Wentworth, and I need you to take charge right now."

Clenching her jaw, Candace glanced toward Ryan. He was jogging toward them now, and she knew with one look at his hard expression that he'd insist she stay put. They didn't have time to argue. Every second the helo sat on the ground gave March and his men time to escape.

I hate this. "Fine." She put her right hand on her hip and shot Ryan a warning glare. "You better take care of her," she shouted over the increasing noise of the Blackhawk's engines.

"Like she was my own sweet grandma," he called back, and held a hand out to beckon Ruby forward.

Candace stood there watching while Ryan jogged her grandma over to the waiting helo and lifted her inside it. Everything in her screamed in denial, demanding that she go with them. It wasn't an option, however.

Stuck here and helpless to do anything to keep her loved ones safe, Candace stood shivering in the cool night air and watched the Blackhawk lift into the inky darkness above the resort. Guilt hit her hard as it flew away. Her stomach sank, and she immediately regretted not being on board.

"Ace, the fire captain needs a word with you. I told him you were the woman in charge."

Heart heavy with worry, she made herself turn around to face Devon, who was standing with Erin and a firefighter in turnout gear by the front entrance. The only thing she could do now was take care of things here on her grandmother's behalf.

"Coming," she called out, and headed toward them.

* * * *

Pulse thudding in his ears, Eric thrust the last of his electronic equipment into his duffel, zipped it up, and hurried to the tunnel entrance. The diversion op had begun more than twenty minutes ago and he hadn't heard a word from Lyle.

Trying one more time to reach the team, he grabbed his radio as he ascended the stairs toward the surface. "Specter, report."

No answer. Just dead air.

Either his men had been captured, or they were dead. Didn't matter which one it was, because he had to get out of here right the hell now.

He hefted the heavy ruck onto his back and picked up both duffels holding enough supplies to get him through the next few days, until he reached the safe house. The perimeter alarm went off just as he neared the upper hatch. He paused, then shoved the heavy steel door upward, because he had no other choice but to run.

A cold breeze whipped over his face as he climbed through into the darkness. The sound of a helo's blades somewhere overhead froze him.

Tipping his head back, he searched the skies and his disbelieving gaze spotted the outline of a Blackhawk against the silver moon as it sped toward him. What the *hell?* The diversion had only begun a little while ago. There was no way any government agency would have had time to respond this fast, let alone pinpoint his location. So who the hell was coming after him?

Fuck. His heart rate shot up. No time to run, and someone might already have seen him. They might track him using his body heat signature. His best chance now was to hide down below, where he knew every inch of the system, and barricade himself inside.

"Specter, I'm pinned down at HQ. Need immediate rescue, over," he said as he climbed back down and secured the steel door overhead. With any luck no one on that helo had seen him. The upper hatch was exposed now, but it couldn't be helped, and nobody knew the location but him and Lyle.

Another perimeter alarm went off when he neared the bottom of the staircase. The area was too heavily wooded for anyone to land a helo near here. Whoever was coming after him must have fast-roped from the helo.

His heart thudded hard in his chest as he knelt and unzipped the duffel, removing grenades and a few blocks of Semtex, then got to work. As of this moment he was trapped like a gopher with a pack of hungry wolves waiting above.

If he was going to die tonight, he would do it fighting for the cause he believed in. One he was prepared to give his life for.

But when the wolves came, they'd find a few unexpected surprises down here. And if he took out enough of them, he just might be able to get out of here, lose them, and win the chance to live and fight another day.

Chapter Eleven

Well, this op was already one for the books and they hadn't even reached their objective yet.

Ryan sat with his back to the wall of the helo with the M4 MacKenzie had given him across his lap, the vibration of the machine familiar and almost soothing. He still didn't know how the guy had pulled a Blackhawk and kit like this out of his damn pocket in the middle of the night. Wade said MacKenzie worked missions like this with the Feds all the time, and Ryan wasn't complaining if it meant the chance to get the man responsible for this attack tonight.

Except for his right shoulder and upper arm hurting like a bitch.

The bleeding had mostly stopped now, but there were areas of numbness down the back of his arm and hand that told him he'd suffered some kind of nerve damage. He flexed his hand, curling the fingers into a fist, noting the diminished strength in his grip.

Fuck it. He could still hold and fire a weapon. This wasn't going to stop him from going after March and his followers who might be hiding out here.

There was just enough moonlight to make out the shape of the land, the thick band of forest as they flew over it. Ruby sat next to him, her short, white hair whipping in the wind, watching the darkened scenery pass by underneath them out the open side door.

He still couldn't believe they'd brought her along, but he

understood the logic behind it. If they couldn't find March's guy, they might have to use her to find the bunker entrance, but only as a last resort. They'd put her in a ballistic vest, just in case, and he could practically feel the excitement humming through her at being included on this op.

She was an odd bird, that was for sure.

"I see the ATV," Cam said, leaning forward to point out the door.

Declan MacKenzie said something to the pilots, and they circled the area. Craning his neck forward, Ryan made out the shape of the ATV left abandoned on the hillside. They used a searchlight to scan the vicinity, but there was no sign of March's second-in-command, Lyle Coventry. Using him to locate the bunker was out.

MacKenzie leaned forward to shout at Ruby. "You're up. Can you get us to that bunker entrance?"

"Yes," she yelled back.

MacKenzie shot him a look, eyebrows raised, and Ryan shrugged. She was the only one of them who knew where the entrance was and she'd actually been there, so she could save them time hunting around. "Worth a shot."

Ruby jabbed him high in the ribs with her elbow, right underneath his wound. He winced and growled in pain. "Sorry," she yelled in his ear, rubbing a hand over his arm in apology. "I forgot."

Breathing deeply until the pain passed, he stared out the open door as the pilots flew them to the rock formation she had mentioned. There was no room for the helo to put down around here, however.

"We gonna fast rope in?" he asked MacKenzie.

The man nodded. "I'll take Ruby."

Sliding down a rope with a bullet wound and diminished grip strength was going to suck, but there was no help for it and they needed to get on the ground quick. After the pilots circled and got them into position above a fairly flat spot in a small clearing, Shane MacKenzie took the role of crew chief and tossed the thick nylon rope out the door.

Cam slid down first, then Jackson, and Wade. Ryan went next, making extra sure he had a solid grip on the rope with his left hand

and feet before easing out of the helo's belly.

He glided down, breathing a sigh of relief when his boots touched solid ground, then held the base of the rope for Declan, who emerged with Ruby. She was wrapped around the front of his torso like a monkey, harnessed against him. Once they were safely on the ground and Ruby unharnessed, Ryan immediately moved away to take up a defensive position with the others.

"We're clear," Declan said a few seconds later via their earpieces. "Pilots are going to pull back a ways to diminish rotor noise and remain on station in case we need a fast pickup. All right, Ruby, point the way."

They fanned out in a single line, Ruby up near the front with Declan, behind Wade and Shane. Ryan mentally shook his head. It was fucking weird, being on an op with Candace's grandma leading them.

Ahead of them in the distance, the grizzly-shaped rock formation loomed in the dim light. They turned left and skirted the base of a rock outcropping.

Not a sound disturbed the silence as they moved. He scanned their surroundings with his NVGs, rifle up and in firing position. His right arm throbbed and ached in protest but he ignored it. The sooner they got to the bunker and ensured it was empty, the sooner he could get patched up properly and get back to Candace.

They must have walked almost two miles in the darkness, snaking through the forest and winding through trees until he was certain Ruby had gotten them lost.

"Over there," he heard her say softly, and turned to follow the end of her finger, pointed to the northwest. "Just around the base of this hill."

"We're getting close," Declan said via their comms. "Heads up for tripwires."

Ryan's gaze swept the ground as they continued closer to the area, then stopped, dropping to one knee with the others while Ruby and Declan hunted around for the entrance.

"Should be right around here," Ruby muttered, walking back and forth. "Gimme those goggle thingies," she said to Declan, holding out a hand impatiently while he undid his helmet and gave it to her.

She looked like something out of a nightmare with the helmet on and the NVGs lowered over her eyes.

"That's better. Now…" She paced to the left a few yards, turned in a half-circle. "Ah! There," she whispered, pointing to a spot a few yards ahead. "See it?"

"I see it," whispered Wade. "I'll be damned."

It took a long moment for Ryan to locate the entrance. They would never have found it without Ruby's help.

Partially hidden by brush, the circular brown steel door was completely camouflaged from view, even half-uncovered the way it was. In this kind of cover, there was no way even a satellite could have found it.

The way the brush had been pushed aside suggested someone had been here recently. Maybe March or that Coventry guy.

Ryan adjusted his grip on his weapon, that familiar buzz at the base of his spine alerting him that danger was near. But he was ready, and while he didn't know either of the MacKenzies, he trusted Wade, Cam, and Jackson to have his back.

Declan took his helmet back and pushed Ruby behind him. "Shane, get her back." His brother took her by the arm and towed her away to the relative safety of a thick stand of trees a hundred feet away while the rest of them moved closer to the entrance.

Ryan hung back with Cam and Jackson while Declan and Wade set a charge on top of the door. Declan moved away a few yards. "You boys ready?"

At their collective affirmative, he blew the charge. A loud bang echoed through the forest, the flash of light illuminating the surrounding trees for an instant before everything went dark again, the landscape lit up in green by their night vision goggles.

Declan approached the steel door, weapon aimed at it in case anyone was waiting below. "Go," he commanded.

Ryan and the others charged forward. Wade raced over as Declan shoved aside the damaged steel hatch and Wade threw in a flashbang.

The moment the diversionary device exploded, shots echoed from somewhere below in the darkened tunnel.

* * * *

Candace stopped in the middle of giving instructions to one of the staff members when the fire marshal walked in through the front doors of the main building. The entire resort was crawling with first responders and FBI agents, and they'd corralled all the guests into the lounge and main dining room, on the off chance that the threat wasn't over yet.

"Fire's out," the forty-something man said as he unstrapped and removed his helmet.

Good. "That's great news. How bad was the damage?"

"Eastern end of the ground and second floors are pretty much a write-off, but the good news is the water and smoke damage to the rest of the building was minimal, and the upper two floors weren't affected."

"I'll have the staff move everyone from the first two floors into other buildings. Any idea how it started?" Had to have been March's men. They'd set it to flush her and the others outside and send them into the ambush.

"Arson investigator is en route, should be here within the hour. He'll be able to tell you for certain once he does his report, but based on what happened here, I'm guessing they doused the side of the building with either gas or lighter fluid and then lit it."

Bastards. Lucky no one had been killed tonight. "Is there anything you need from me right now?" She was already juggling several balls at the moment, but she could handle one more.

His lips quirked, his brown eyes kind. "Other than you going to the hospital to get that wound checked out? No."

She smiled at him, even though smiling was the last thing she felt like doing. There'd been no word on the mission status. She'd refused to let his firefighters or the paramedics tend to her. Erin knew what she was doing, and had patched her up just fine until she could get to the hospital. The outer edge of her left shoulder blade ached, yeah, and she would go get it checked out by a doctor later.

"I will." But not until Ryan was back safe and sound. Until then, she wasn't budging from this resort.

He nodded once. "I'll let you get back to work, then. Looks like you've got your hands full."

At least being busy gave her something to focus on other than worrying about Ryan and her grandma.

After instructing the staff to move everyone from the damaged lower rooms to new ones and give the guests something to eat, she hurried to the lounge to inform everyone what was going on. Erin and Dev were both there taking care of the guests with the rest of the staff, serving coffee and tea and whatever snacks they'd managed to find in the kitchens.

"Any word on what's happening?" Dev asked her quietly over in the corner of the room a minute later.

"Not yet, but I'm going to get a status update now. If I find out anything, I'll let you guys know."

"All right."

Exhaustion pulled at her, the pain in her side making her even more edgy as she exited the main building and headed for the adjoining one to the west. The Feds had set up a command post of sorts in the grill restaurant.

She spotted Maya standing next to one of them, deep in conversation. Her friend's gaze cut to her as Candace approached.

"Is there a status update?" Candace asked without preamble.

The stocky, middle-aged FBI agent beside Maya shook his head. "Not yet."

She didn't believe him, and glanced at Maya for verification. Maya shook her head and Candace tamped down her impatience. "Are they at the bunker yet?"

"Yes," Maya answered. "But that's all I know."

Great. Expelling a deep breath, Candace raked a hand through her hair. "How long until we can expect an update?" she asked the man.

"I'll let you know as soon as I can."

"You look ready to drop," Maya said, catching her right hand and towing her toward an empty table. "Sit. I'll get you something to drink."

She sat, glowering. "I don't want anything to drink. I want a damn status update." *At least tell me they're still okay.*

"Yeah, you and me both, *chica.*" Maya shot the male agent a dark look, hands on her trim hips. "Unfortunately, we're shit out of luck on that front for the time being."

* * * *

Pulling the steel door shut behind him, Eric loaded a fresh magazine into his rifle and paused at the entrance of his safe room. His hands were steady, his heart rate only slightly elevated as he waited in the darkness, not even a hint of ambient light filtering through his NVGs.

They were here, although he didn't know how many. He'd known they were here even before they'd hit the entrance door with explosives and tossed in the stun grenade.

His perimeter alarm had alerted him of their arrival minutes beforehand, allowing him plenty of time to set the last of his surprises and retreat here. If the men coming after him were highly trained and experienced, then the booby traps wouldn't stop them.

But they would buy Eric time.

Lyle had never reported back after the attack, so Eric had to assume he'd been captured or killed. He was on his own now, but maybe it was better this way.

His turf. His terms.

His way.

They could try to take him alive but he'd kill as many of them as he could first. And he wasn't afraid to die.

They wouldn't kill him though. That would only make him a martyr to his followers, fueling the momentum of the movement he'd begun. Keeping him in prison was equally dangerous, because he could recruit from within the prison system and his followers would continue to operate without him. His men were loyal to him, and to their cause.

No matter what happened tonight, he won.

A loud boom rent the air, shaking the tunnel so much that the walls and floor trembled around him.

He smiled in the darkness. His first diversion.

Surprise, assholes.

And there were more where that came from. They thought they

had him trapped down here, but they were wrong. If he played this right, soon they'd be the ones trapped, while he escaped right out from underneath them.

He flexed his fingers around his weapon, ready for the coming showdown. "Now come and get me."

Chapter Twelve

Ryan dove to the ground when the explosion from inside the tunnel shattered the stillness.

Ears ringing, right arm screaming in protest, he shook his head to clear it and looked around. All the others had hit the deck as well, but thankfully no one seemed to be hurt.

"Everyone good?" MacKenzie said.

"Yeah," Ryan muttered, gritting his teeth as he pushed to his feet. Jesus, whatever that was had packed one hell of a punch. March had to be down there somewhere, must have triggered it somehow. Why else set booby traps if not to protect himself? "He's waiting for us."

"Let's go."

Ryan followed behind the others, carefully easing his way into the circular opening to climb down the metal rungs anchored into the concrete wall. He kept his right hand on his rifle, to stabilize his weapon and keep from moving his arm around more than necessary. The patch job was holding for the most part but he could feel blood trickling down his side. Must have re-opened it when he hit the ground a minute ago.

When his boots touched the floor he turned and began walking down a concrete tunnel. The farther they moved away from the entrance, the less light there was for his NVGs to pick up.

Taking point, MacKenzie led the way down the corridor, their steps echoing off the walls. The place was damn creepy and Ryan couldn't believe Ruby had spent time down here. They passed the spot where the first booby trap had gone off, the walls, floor, and ceiling peppered with pockmarks.

"Son of a bitch," MacKenzie murmured, stopping a dozen yards or so ahead. "He's got this whole section wired up to blow."

"Wentworth and I can help you," Wade said, stepping forward. Ryan stepped around Cam and Jackson, leaving them to provide over watch, and moved closer to the other two.

What he saw made his heart sink.

March or whoever was down here had crisscrossed wires across the width of the tunnel before them, like a massive silver spider web, punctuated with at least a dozen frag grenades.

"If he was ready to blow this up, then he's either not here, or he's got another tunnel to escape from." And it was going to take them precious time to render this inert so they could get past it.

MacKenzie nodded and contacted Shane to confirm with Ruby. "She says there were five different exit routes when she was here."

"Great," Ryan muttered, hunkering down and fishing a pair of wire cutters out of his vest while Wade aimed a penlight and helped him figure out where to cut. Even with the three of them working feverishly it took almost ten minutes to undo everything and set the grenades aside where they wouldn't pose further threat.

MacKenzie waved them forward. They found two more booby traps, and had to stop and dismantle them before moving on. Ryan's entire upper right arm ached, the trickle of blood sticky against his side. The tunnel forked right, then left, then right again. Zig-zagging its way under the mountain.

At a pile of rubble blocking one side of it, they stopped. "Another tunnel?" Ryan murmured.

"Yep," Wade confirmed.

Looked like what Ruby had said before might be true. Maybe the government had destroyed part of the complex or filled some of it in, but since then someone else had cleared part of it back out again.

Twenty yards down the main tunnel, they found the entrance to another. Ryan's heart rate picked up as they checked the door and eased inside. He, Wade, and MacKenzie went in to check it out. They hit a dead end a hundred and fifty feet in and retraced their steps.

"Keep going," MacKenzie told them all, and continued down the main tunnel.

In the glow of the penlight Wade aimed ahead, they saw the end of it. The entire forward section of the tunnel was caved in, rubble obliterating the entrance from floor to ceiling. But there was one final door a few feet away from it to their right.

MacKenzie waved them forward, stopping to check the door. Ryan flexed his fingers around the grips of his weapon, the butt snug against the front of his sore shoulder. The door didn't look rigged, but opening it was a gamble.

Ryan stayed to the right of it as MacKenzie moved to its left and reached for the lever. He strained to twist it, the groan of metal on metal echoing in the tunnel, scraping over his nerve endings.

It opened slightly. Wade tossed in another flashbang. It exploded with a bright flash of light and a loud burst that pulsed against his eardrums. Then, nothing but silence.

Wade went in first this time, then MacKenzie and Ryan. Nothing but empty black space lay ahead of them. Then came the faint sound of footsteps from somewhere behind them.

"Shit, someone's moving the other way," Cam said.

Ryan rushed back out of the side tunnel with the others, the sound of someone running fading ahead of them in the distance. "He's going for the main shaft."

"And he'll try to bury us all down here if we don't stop him before he gets there," MacKenzie muttered, saying exactly what Ryan had feared.

Fuck! The grenades. They'd left the goddamn grenades lying there. March could use them to pin them all down here, maybe even take a few of them out, then blow the tunnel entrance shut.

He ran back the way they'd come, right on Wade's heels, MacKenzie behind him, then Cam and Jackson. They had to stop this fucker before he reached the grenades.

The darkness hampered them until Wade switched on the tac light on his weapon, flooding the tunnel with a beam of light. Ryan's pulse thudded in his ears, the pain in his arm disappearing under the rush of fear and adrenaline. They were literally in a race for their lives and couldn't afford to lose.

His boots thudded on the concrete floor with every step. Shots exploded down the tunnel. Bullets sprayed the floor and walls, bouncing all over, making them draw back into a huddle behind the bend in the wall for cover.

Then something metallic pinged off the floor up ahead. His heart seized.

"Grenade!" He dove to the ground, climbing half on top of Wade out of instinct to shield his teammate an instant before it detonated. Bits of concrete and dust pelted them but there was no sharp, hot bite of metal.

A vision of Candace appeared in his head. Laughing at something he'd said, her head thrown back, dark eyes dancing. Then he thought of her beautiful face crumpling with grief if he died tonight. He was *not* going to be buried alive down here.

Ryan lifted his head, surged to his feet, and ran headlong after Wade, determined to get the son of a bitch waiting up ahead. Just as they came to the last bend in the tunnel, another grenade rattled and rolled its way toward them.

They hit the ground again. Ryan bit back a howl of pain as red-hot agony swept up his right arm.

He vaguely saw Wade tossing his own grenade before hitting the floor on his belly. The two weapons detonated at almost the same moment, the combined concussion ringing his head and compressing his lungs.

"Think I hit him," he heard Wade say, and clambered to his feet once more to give chase. The pain made his vision waver but he shook it off.

In the beam of light from Wade's weapon, Ryan saw March up ahead. Just a blur of motion as he started up the metal rungs in the concrete wall.

Everything slowed down to a fraction of normal time. His gaze locked on March's hand as the man reached for the pin in another grenade.

He raised the muzzle of his weapon at the same time Wade did, aiming center mass before firing. They hit him dead in the chest, knocking him off the ladder. He fell, hitting the ground with a solid thud.

MacKenzie raced past them, weapon up. "Don't fucking move, asshole," he warned.

Ryan was right behind him, kicking away the man's rifle as MacKenzie searched him for other weapons. Their bullets had hit March right in the center of his ballistic vest. He gasped for breath as MacKenzie rolled him over and secured his hands behind him.

It was only then that Ryan realized how fast he was breathing, how amped up he was. He wanted to smash March's face in with his bare fist for what the man had done. For wounding Candace, for wounding and almost killing him and his teammates down here.

"Mother *fucker.*"

Jaw clenched, he slung his weapon across his back and began climbing up the metal rungs of the ladder anchored into the concrete wall. Near the top he paused. "Shane, how we looking up there?" he murmured into the mic.

"All clear. You guys coming up?"

"Affirmative." Without the adrenaline masking the pain, his arm was now aching like a bitch. He grimaced as he climbed his way to the top, and by the time he got there he was covered in sweat. Biting back a groan, he crawled over the edge of the opening and stayed on one knee to catch his breath.

A solid hand landed on his left shoulder. "You good?" Cam.

"Yeah. Just need a second."

"I got movement outside the tunnel entrance," Shane reported, voice sharp. "Single heat signature, lost it in the trees to the southeast—"

The rest of what he said was lost under the roar of blood in Ryan's ears.

He was already dropping to his stomach, rolling behind a slight knoll to take cover. As soon as he was in place he aimed at the far tree line, and a bullet punched into the metal hatch two feet in front of him with a loud ping.

"Fucker," Cam snarled under his breath, flat on his belly beside Ryan.

"You guys got him?" Declan said over their comms, still inside the tunnel.

Ryan lay unmoving, eye to his scope, every muscle tense as he scanned those trees. "I got nothing. Shane?"

"Moving around to get another look."

"Ruby—"

"She's good."

Was it Coventry out there shooting at them sniper-style? Or was it another of March's men? "Any other heat signatures?"

"Negative, just the one."

For now, anyway. Ryan eased the barrel of his weapon farther to the right.

A flash of movement caught his attention through the trees. "I got him. Hundred-and-twenty yards, two o'clock."

"You got a shot?" Wade said, inside the tunnel with the others.

"Negative. We're gonna have to flush the bastard out," he muttered.

"Roger that," Declan answered. "Shane, you cover the left flank. Ryan, you and Cam take the right and we'll come up and take the middle."

"Wilco." The right side of his undershirt was stiff with blood. More of it pooled warm against his ribs. *Sooner you get this bastard, the sooner you can get that plugged again.*

"Ready?" Cam whispered.

"Yeah. I'll cover you."

Cam shot up and ran to the right while Ryan watched the trees for more movement. Another shot rang out. Cam cursed but kept running. "To my left," he reported, dropping behind the cover of a big boulder.

Ryan used his left arm to push to his knees, waited for Cam's soft *go* before racing after him. No more shots echoed in the silence, but Ryan glimpsed a tiny shift in the underbrush ahead and to the left as he ran. "I got him." Dropping onto one knee, he took aim, fired. Then he waited.

"I see him," Shane reported. "To the left of your position."

Ryan eased the barrel of his weapon to the left, consciously slowing his heart rate. *Come on, asshole. Move.*

A branch swayed in his night vision goggles. He aimed at it and fired.

"You winged him, but he's not down," Shane said. "I can't get a clear shot, but he's moving deeper into the woods now."

Not for long.

With Cam backing him up, Ryan raced across the open space and into the trees, just in time to see someone stumbling ahead of them about forty yards in the distance. He and Cam both fired at the same time. The man grunted and toppled over, disappearing from view.

"He's down and not moving," Shane confirmed. "You're clear."

Ryan lowered his rifle, staying close on Cam's heels as his teammate ran for the body. Breathing hard, covered in sweat, Ryan followed him to where the man's corpse was sprawled out on the forest floor. One bullet had gone through the base of his neck, severing his spinal column. The other had hit him in the upper back.

The man was lying on his stomach, eyes open, no movement in his torso. Ryan knelt down, took off his left glove and checked the pulse, just to confirm. "Dead." He rose to his feet and slipped his right hand into his pocket to give his aching arm a rest.

The pain eased a mere fraction. He rubbed his left hand over his face, suddenly exhausted. God, what a night. Now that this was over, all he wanted to do was get back to Candace and go lie down with her in their room, hold her as close as he could. Unfortunately it would be a while before he could do that.

MacKenzie came up a minute later and looked down at the body. "That's Coventry."

Ryan relaxed. So the immediate threat had been neutralized. Together they walked out of the trees to find Jackson and Wade guarding March.

"How's that patch job holding up, Went?" Cam asked, sticking a penlight in his mouth to have a look.

"Not too well."

"Nope," Cam confirmed around the light, and started pulling fresh bandages out of the kit he'd brought with him from the helo.

Ryan hissed in a breath when his buddy peeled the bloody bandage away from the wound to put another QuikClot one over it. His eyes watered at the cruel burn. Dammit, that *hurt*. "You know what, Sandberg?"

One hand gripping their prisoner's upper arm, Wade looked

over at him.

"I'm *never* coming to another wedding of yours. Ever. So next time, don't bother inviting me."

"Yeah, and not Jackson or me either," said Cam, pressing hard on the bandage to slow the bleeding. Ryan bit back a curse.

Wade grinned, his teeth flashing white in the pale moonlight. "Guess it's a good thing I'm only doing this once then, huh?"

Yeah, a damn good thing. Especially since Erin was a total sweetheart.

Declan requested the pilots to move in to extract them and grabbed March by his bound wrists to shove him forward and down the hill. Jackson stepped closer to Ryan, aiming the beam of the flashlight at him.

A flurry of movement to the left caught his attention as Shane and Ruby appeared out of the trees. Shane hustled over to his brother and shoved March to his knees.

"Anyone got their phone handy so they can get this on video?" Declan asked, aiming a flashlight into the prisoner's face.

"Right here," Ryan answered, reaching his left hand into one of his vest pockets to fish out his phone. "Smile pretty," he said to March, then hit record and nodded at Declan to begin.

"Is that him?" Ruby demanded in a pissed-off tone as she made her way up the hill. The years of smoking unfiltered cigarettes didn't seem to have affected her lung capacity any. She was storming toward them at a pretty impressive clip for someone her age.

"Uh, yes ma'am," Jackson answered when no one else did.

Ryan looked up from his phone's screen as Ruby stormed straight for March. The man's head came up and even from where he stood, Ryan could see the guy's eyes widen in alarm.

"Whoa," he said to Cam, who was still poking and prodding at the wound. Suddenly the pain in Ryan's arm wasn't so bad anymore. Now he was even more glad he'd brought his phone with him.

Not even bothering to fight the grin spreading across his face, Ryan stood back and kept recording, eagerly waiting for the show to start.

Chapter Thirteen

The moment she heard the rotors, Candace got up off the chair she'd been sitting on inside the lobby and ran out onto the north lawn. Maya, Dev, and Erin followed, along with the cops and Feds they'd already spoken to.

She held her breath as the outline of the helo came into view. They'd had zero updates since Ryan and the others had left, and she'd spent the past ninety-some-odd minutes worrying that something had gone wrong. They'd gone in there with no backup, and with her grandmother of all people in tow.

She winced as she shifted the sling Erin had made for her out of a bed sheet to minimize the strain on her shoulder blade, eyes glued to the helo. Was everyone okay? Did they get March?

The Blackhawk circled overhead then came in to land on the far side of the lawn. Moments later, shadowy shapes began to climb out of the interior. The first one was escorting another person. Someone wearing a hood.

The Feds near her took off running toward them, and she realized it was Declan MacKenzie with a prisoner. March?

She looked past them to the helo, recognizing her grandma's petite form as someone led her across the lawn, her short white hair whipping in the rotor wash. The worry eased a little, but not completely as she searched for Ryan.

Two more men hopped out, then her heart did a painful somersault in her chest when Ryan's tall, familiar form finally jumped out of the helo.

Without waiting, she raced for him. He ran toward her, caught her with his good arm and dragged her close, his hand locked around the back of her head as he pressed her cheek to his chest. "I'm good, baby, I'm okay."

"You swear?" she asked, squeezing him for all she was worth with her right arm.

"I swear. How are you?" He pulled back to study her, his hand solid around the back of her neck.

"Relieved," she answered, tipping her face up to kiss him, clutching at the back of his tac vest because she couldn't make herself let him go yet. "They wouldn't tell us shit about what was going on. Was that March?"

"Yeah."

She looked over her shoulder to see the Feds hauling him off to a waiting vehicle, MacKenzie with them. She faced her husband. "Are you still bleeding?"

"Just a little."

In other words, yes. "I want you to go to the hospital."

Surprisingly, he didn't argue. "Yeah, okay. Come on, let's get you back inside where it's warm."

Holding tight to his hand, she walked back with him to the main building and stopped outside in front of the lobby. Her friends were all waiting there, hugging their significant others.

In the light from the lamp post behind them, Candace pulled back to scan Ryan for injuries, but aside from the blood on his right upper arm, he seemed okay. The awful knot in her stomach finally eased. "So it's over?"

"Our part is," he answered, bending to kiss her again. "The Feds will take it from here."

Good. "Did Grandma go with you guys on the ground?"

"Just to the tunnel entrance, but yeah." His eyes twinkled, his lips curving upward. "The best part of the whole night was when she went after March."

She blinked. "What do you mean?"

Now he grinned. "She slapped him."

Hardly able to believe what she'd just heard, Candace released Ryan from the one-armed hug she'd been giving him and gaped up at him in astonishment. In the soft light his eyes twinkled and she couldn't tell if he was being serious or not.

"She *slapped* him? Like, literally slapped him?" Getting shot freaking *hurt*, so she was glad to have a distraction until Jackson brought the car around to take them to the hospital.

"Damn near smacked his face right off," he said with pride, the pain and fatigue easing from his features as he grinned. "I got it on video. Gotta delete it once I show it to you though, for legal reasons. Don't want this being used as evidence." Looking enormously pleased with himself, he pulled his phone out of his vest pocket, wincing as the motion pulled at his wound.

"Careful, you're gonna undo all of Cam's work," she admonished.

"Yeah, I think I'm done using my right arm for a bit," he agreed, holding up the phone in his left hand.

"I wanna see," Maya said, sidling up behind them to put her hands on Candace's waist.

"Me too." Dev and Erin came over to peer around either of her shoulders, all of them standing huddled together in the chilly fall night air.

She was grateful to have her friends around her. While Ryan and the guys had been out hunting the shooters, her girls had done everything humanly possible to take care of her and distract her from the pain and worry. They'd all given statements to the police and FBI agents who had responded to the attack, so at least that part was done.

She slid her right arm around Ryan's waist and leaned into his solid build. Even though she hated hospitals and wasn't looking forward to being poked and prodded anymore tonight, at least she'd get a reprieve from this whole situation for a little while, and get some quiet time with him on the way there and back.

The video finally loaded and Ryan angled the phone for them all to see, then hit play. He'd filmed it from a ways back, so it was a little grainy, and the lighting wasn't great. But it was definitely Eric March who knelt before the MacKenzie brothers with his hands bound behind his back, one eye swollen shut and blood dripping from his nose.

Candace's lips compressed. *Asshole.*

"Is that him?" her grandmother's voice snapped out, somewhere off screen.

Uh oh. She recognized that tone. And it meant trouble for whoever was about to be on the receiving end of her temper. She bit her lip in anticipation, dying to see what happened next, the burning and throbbing beneath her left shoulder blade seeming a little more tolerable now.

"Uh, yes ma'am," Jackson responded, from somewhere near Ryan.

A second later, Ruby Bradford came into view. Candace put her right hand over her mouth to smother a laugh at the sight of her tiny grandmother, dressed in a ballistic vest and a sweat suit ten sizes too big for her that someone must have loaned her, because earlier she'd been wearing just a silk kimono.

On screen she stalked her way over to March, her expression livid. Candace had been the target of that look a couple times when she was a kid when she'd gotten lippy or stepped too far out of line, and had learned to fear it.

March must have realized he was in deep shit too, because he lifted his head and blinked up at her in astonishment as she stopped and stood glowering down at him, hands fisted at her sides.

"You bastard! Burning my resort and then shooting my granddaughter and her husband? Well, you picked the wrong damn target, you pathetic, sniveling, cowardly son of a traitorous bitch!"

Behind March, both MacKenzie brothers grinned. A split second later her grandma reared one arm back, letting out a mighty grunt as she swung her open palm across March's left cheek with a resounding crack that snapped his face around.

Candace gasped and March jerked his head back in shock. "What the *fuck?*"

Even from the distance Ryan had filmed at, Candace could see her grandmother's eyes bug out at his language. Ruby Bradford swore all the time, but someone using that kind of language in front of her was a definite no-no.

"You watch your filthy mouth, criminal!" She backhanded him across the other cheek, and, apparently incensed now, kept on slapping him. Four, five, six mighty blows while March tried to dodge the strikes, his only defense curling into himself before Shane MacKenzie finally stepped in and grabbed her around the waist from behind, a giant smirk on his face.

Her grandma struggled in his grip, still yelling threats at March, but even as Shane picked her up off the ground to carry her out of range, she twisted and lashed out with a booted foot, catching March in the jaw.

His head snapped back and he shouted in pain before yelling at Declan. "God dammit, get that crazy old lady the fuck *away* from me!"

Whatever Declan said was drowned out by her grandmother's shouted threats and Ryan's rolling laughter. The video ended and Candace looked up at her husband to see a huge grin on his face as he wiped away tears of mirth with the back of his left hand.

"Fucking *awesome*." He laughed again and Candace couldn't help but join in, which was messed up, considering they'd both been shot and were in more pain than either one of them wanted to admit.

"Wow, I've never seen her like that. She was seriously pissed off," Candace murmured, glad for the lightened mood the video had brought. She gasped as an idea occurred to her. "We gotta send that to my dad!"

"Sorry, no can do. That was a one-time viewing opportunity," he said, and deleted it. "She sprained her wrist on that third slap, but still kept on going. Jackson wrapped it up for her on the flight back. We had to keep her separated from March, just in case, but even with him hooded and bound at the front of the aircraft she kept glaring holes at him all the way back."

That was Grandma. She could hold a grudge like nobody's business, too. And once someone won her love and loyalty, those emotions were just as fierce as her temper.

Smiling fondly, Candace looked around. "Where is she, anyway?" Last time Candace had seen her grandma, she'd been talking to Declan MacKenzie.

"In the bar. MacKenzie boys are buying her the first of what I'm sure will be several rounds of drinks, and once this story gets out, I doubt she'll ever have to buy any booze or cigarettes of her own ever again. She's a fucking legend now." He shook his head. "I gained a whole new level of respect and fear of her tonight. I've never heard language like that come from a woman her age's mouth before." Another grin. "It was epic."

Maya squeezed her right shoulder. "Your grandma really is the shit, Ace," she said, laughing.

"Yeah. She totally is." She turned to Ryan. "Can we get going to the hospital now?" She hated hospitals and wasn't looking forward to what would happen there but she knew her husband, and wouldn't accept that he was "fine" until a doctor said so.

"Yeah." He caught her right hand and tugged her close for a hard kiss, a smile pulling at his full lips. "You're the shit too, by the way," he murmured, his voice full of admiration.

She gave him a saucy grin just as headlights swung around the end of the circular roundabout in the driveway, signaling Jackson's arrival. "Thanks. It's genetic."

* * * *

As predicted, the hospital visit was no fun at all. They updated her tetanus shot and gave her antibiotics to take, then re-bandaged Erin's handiwork and gave her some mild painkillers that she wasn't too proud to swallow.

X-rays had shown she had no fractures but Ryan had a hairline one in his upper right humerus, and he'd also suffered some minor radial nerve damage. The doctors had no way of predicting whether it was permanent, or to what extent it would affect his ability to perform his job. They'd know more once the swelling went down and he healed up.

"How you holding up, sweetheart?"

She looked up from her seat outside the x-ray room as Ryan walked down the linoleum hallway toward her, his right arm immobilized in a sling. "Okay so far. You?"

He made a face and lowered himself into the chair beside her.

"Tonight wasn't the most fun I ever had."

"Yeah, no kidding," she agreed, leaning sideways to rest her head on his uninjured shoulder.

He tucked his heavy arm around her waist, careful not to bump her left side, and kissed the top of her head. They were alone here in the hallway, with only the occasional nurse or tech walking past. "You really okay?" he murmured.

She wasn't going to lie. "Tonight definitely stirred up a lot of stuff for me."

He made a soft sound of reassurance and tightened his hand around her waist. "I'll bet."

It had been on her mind all night. "It confirmed my decision to leave the force, that's for sure." She was done with guns and violence and anything remotely resembling combat. "And I hated being left behind while you went on the op. I felt helpless, was worried sick about you the whole time you were gone."

"I was fine," he murmured against the top of her head. "I had Cam, Jackson, and Wade there to watch my back, along with MacKenzie."

"I don't care who you were with, I was still worried. I realized tonight that it's way easier on me when I don't know the specifics of what's going on when you go out on an op."

She paused for a moment, considering her next words carefully. "The one good thing about tonight's situation was that it brought certain things about my life into sudden, crystal clarity." She lifted her head from his shoulder and stared into his eyes. "You're my number one priority. No question. Sometimes I feel like I come in last in your life, though, and I need to feel like I matter to you more than your job or country does."

Shock filled his expression. "Sweetheart, of course I love you more than my job or my country. Hell, you're my motivation when I'm out there on a mission." He sounded totally bewildered, as though her viewpoint had come out of left field. "When things get tough, I think of you and it makes all the shit that happens bearable."

That made her smile. "You do?"

"Hell, yes."

She curled into him more, closed her eyes, and breathed in his comforting scent. "I love you." She swallowed and dug down for the courage to say her worst fear aloud. "I couldn't take it if I lost you."

His arm tightened around her. "You won't lose me. Not ever," he murmured against the top of her head. "I'll always come home to you."

He meant it; she could hear the conviction in his voice. But there was no way he could guarantee that promise.

They were both quiet as Maya and Jackson drove them back to the resort, Candace snuggled in as close as she could get. Thankfully the cops and FBI agents had all left except for the ones staying for security purposes with MacKenzie's crew, so they didn't have to do any more interviews.

She held Ryan's hand on the way up to the new room they'd been given on a different floor where there was no smoke or water damage, relieved to be alone and have this nightmarish night over with. All she wanted was to curl up against her husband and spend the rest of the night in his arms. Or arm, as it were.

The air in the hallway still smelled faintly of smoke but fortunately the sprinkler system and the fire crews had long since managed to put the fire out on the first floor before it had damaged more than the lower two floors. Erin and Wade still wanted the wedding to go ahead as scheduled at eleven in the morning, so they all needed to get some rest.

After gingerly peeling her T-shirt off, she paused before the mirror and angled so she could see her bandage at the edge of her left shoulder blade. Dark blue and purple bruises were already spreading out from under the edges. At least the pills they'd given her had taken the edge off the pain.

"Do you think my gown will hide this well enough?" she asked Ryan, who had stripped and was already lying in bed on his side, watching her, his wounded arm bound up in a sling across his wide, muscular chest.

"Yeah, probably. Come lie down with me."

She loathed the thought of everyone staring at her while she was up there, whispering about what had happened, but she'd do anything for Erin. Including standing at the altar in a few hours while nursing a bullet wound that hurt every bit as much as she'd imagined.

Exhausted, she crossed to the bed, climbed in beside him, and lay facing him on her uninjured side. He looked just as tired as she felt and she could tell he was hurting a lot more than he let on.

Reaching out, she cupped the side of his face and rubbed her thumb over his cheek. She would have leaned forward to kiss him but it would hurt too much so she stayed put. Searching his eyes, she sighed. "We look like the saddest bookends in the world right now."

He snorted out a laugh. "Yeah, we sure do."

And it said a lot that he wasn't trying to initiate anything. She traced her fingers over his face, wishing she could take his pain away. "Who knew the mountains in Montana could be even more dangerous than the ones in Afghanistan?"

"I know." His face grew serious and he slipped his left hand beneath her to wind it around her nape, fingers gently digging into her sore muscles. "Do you know how much I love you?"

A smile tugged at her mouth and her heart squeezed. He'd obviously been thinking about what she'd said at the hospital. "I think so, yes."

He stared into her eyes, the raw emotion there making her throat tighten. "I could have lost you tonight. Until we talked earlier I never realized how much I've been taking you for granted, even though I didn't mean to. I don't ever want you to think I don't love you or appreciate every single thing you do for us, whether I'm here or away."

Her throat tightened. He was such a ham all the time; this level of seriousness and his heartfelt words showed just how much tonight had scared him. How the thought of losing her scared him.

With a soft smile she slipped her right arm beneath him and around the back of his neck. She snuggled in close to his body, savoring his warmth and strength, the feel of his love surrounding her like a healing balm. "Nobody's perfect, but you come pretty damn close to being perfect for me."

The corner of his mouth tipped upward. "Good. Now let's try to get some sleep, huh?"

"Okay." She doubted either of them was going to get much of it, but it was a huge comfort just to be able to curl up with him for the rest of the night.

Planting a slow, firm kiss on her lips, he grimaced as he reached past her head to turn off the wall sconce beside the bed. Then he pulled her close with his good arm and held her, their hearts beating in unison in the darkened room.

Chapter Fourteen

The morning of the wedding was cool and bright, barely a cloud in the sky. Ryan glanced away from the window in their room and winced as he draped the right side of his jacket over his sling, the motion pulling at his stitches.

It had been an uncomfortable few hours of rest for both him and Candace. Neither of them had wanted to stop touching the other, so it meant a lot of awkward positioning to make it work. He hadn't slept much and neither had Candace, but she'd had to be up and gone by nine to get ready with the rest of the bridesmaids, no matter how sore and shitty she felt.

He felt bad that she had to soldier through a wedding when she should have spent the day in bed resting and letting him pamper her with cuddles and room service. They'd do that as soon as the reception was over, he decided.

His entire right shoulder and side hurt and he was damn glad he didn't have to stand up there in front of everyone during the wedding. In the shower earlier, he'd been covered in bright purple and magenta bruises. He'd refused to take the pills he'd gotten at the hospital, because they made him feel woozy and sick to his stomach, so he had to get through this cold turkey.

When he got downstairs a few minutes later, the lobby was already filled with wedding guests. Around the perimeter he spotted several of the security guards MacKenzie had brought in to watch the place, but they were doing a good job of blending in. Declan was personally seeing to the security of the wedding party and guests, as well as keeping the media away from the resort.

Not surprisingly, news outlets across the country were already streaming stories about last night's attack by an apparent domestic terror cell, and that a senator's daughter had been among the victims. Thankfully Candace's name and family hadn't been leaked yet, but it wouldn't stay that way for long.

Jackson stood near the entrance and nodded when he saw Ryan, a smile tugging at his mouth. "Hey, big guy. How you feeling?"

"I feel awesome."

"Uh huh." He gestured outside. "Want to go get our seats before this gets rolling?"

"Yeah." He slipped on his shades as they stepped outside into the bright, late morning sunlight. "Maya hear anything yet?"

"She's been in contact with her people at the Bureau. Apparently March had been building a militia with the hopes of attacking government targets in Montana and elsewhere, eventually planning to hit D.C. His big plan was to have his followers rise up and topple the government, thought the country would rise up against the so-called 'tyranny his ancestors and fellow brothers and sisters in arms' had fought against."

"Wow, he wasn't into small potatoes, was he?"

"Nope. The Feds aren't releasing March's name just yet, but it won't be long. Not sure if they've got him talking yet but they're tracking down all his followers as we speak, and apparently there've already been a fair number rounded up. March Madness is dead." He shot Ryan a sidelong glance. "How's Ace holding up?"

"So far so good. Looking at her right now, you'd never know she was shot last night." He broke into a smile when he saw her standing off to the side of the white gazebo set into the middle of the garden, talking to Devon and Maya, all in their bridesmaids dresses.

"Yeah, she looks good."

She sure as hell did. The soft peach gown made her skin glow, and the sunlight glinted off her golden-blond hair. She'd carefully tucked the bandage beneath the edge of the fabric where it crossed her shoulder blade, and what the dress didn't hide of the bruising she'd managed to cover with makeup.

Watching her now, a powerful tide of love and protectiveness flowed through him. She meant everything to him, and as much as being wounded sucked for them both, it meant he'd have more time stateside with her while he healed up. After all this he wanted time alone to reconnect with her without any interruptions or distractions. To show her how much he loved her, how much she meant to him.

"Went, Thatcher."

They both turned their heads to find Liam and Honor Magrath heading their way across the lawn. Liam wore a dark suit and Honor had on a pale green dress. "Hey, you guys made it after all."

"Just in time." The Night Stalker pilot took in Ryan's sling and offered him his left hand to shake.

Apparently not satisfied with a mere handshake, Honor wrapped her arms around Ryan's waist instead, her pale blue eyes searching his. "We just heard what happened. Are you all right?"

"I'm okay."

"And Ace?"

"See for yourself." He nodded toward Candace.

Honor's strawberry-blond hair swished around her shoulders as she turned her head toward Candace, then back to him. "Okay, now I feel better."

Liam set an arm around her shoulders, looking at him and Jackson. "Sorry I missed out on the action. I hear you guys had one hell of a hunting expedition last night."

"Yeah, we did." Ryan looked around. "Where's Cam?"

"He'll be here in a sec." Jackson nodded toward the neatly-arranged rows of white folding chairs set out on the lawn in front of the gazebo. "Shall we?"

Violin music started up a minute after they'd sat down, signaling the start of the ceremony. He half turned in his seat to watch Wade stride down the grassy aisle with his groomsmen and stand at the entrance of the gazebo dressed in a black tux and Stetson to await his bride.

Next came the bridesmaids. He couldn't take his eyes off his wife. She glowed up there at the front of the line of bridesmaids, tall and gorgeous and strong, giving no sign of the pain he knew she was in.

Damn, she amazed him. When this was over, he was going to take her away someplace to relax. Somewhere with a white sand beach and their own private hideaway within sight of the ocean, where they could be alone and enjoy each other's company.

When everyone was at the altar, Maya appeared at the top of the aisle, looking shockingly soft and feminine in her matron of honor gown. She walked down to take her place directly next to the altar, and faced front to await the bride.

After a pause the violinist began a new song and Erin stepped into view, her arm linked through her father's. Even through the veil Ryan could see the tears in her eyes and the tremulous smile on her mouth as she walked toward Wade.

He smiled. Those two had gone through hell together too. Ryan was damn glad they were getting the chance to have a happily ever after.

During the vows, Ryan watched his wife, reminded of their own wedding last year. There had been hundreds of guests there, most of whom he hadn't even known, and the whole thing had been over-the-top in his opinion, but he still remembered the important things. The way Candace had looked in that gorgeous ivory gown, the way her hand had gripped his during the vows...and every single promise they'd made to each other that day.

Even though she knew he loved her and he'd tried to show her how much, Ryan had to admit he hadn't been the greatest husband so far. Like she'd said, he'd let her down, and that still bothered him. He'd never meant to make her feel alone or insignificant. He was going to work way harder to be there for her emotionally going forward.

She'd known what she was getting with him and his job when they'd gotten married, and she'd stood by him. His career meant he was away from her for long stretches at a time, but from now on when he did have the chance to talk to her, whether by phone or computer, he would try harder to love her the way she deserved.

A second honeymoon was exactly what the doctor ordered for them. Now that they were both recuperating from gunshot wounds, getting away for an extended trip was even more important. Time to heal and have the chance to fall in love with each other all over again.

He'd romance her so much she wouldn't even know what hit her.

Sounded like a hell of a plan to him.

Erin and Wade finished their vows and sealed them with a long, definitely *not* PG kiss that had the audience whistling and cheering. As soon as they disappeared up the aisle, with Maya, Candace, Dev and the others trailing behind, Ryan followed.

When the blessedly short receiving line wound to a close, he snagged his wife's hand and took her to a private corner around the side of the main building. He wanted to be alone with her for a few minutes.

"What did you think?" she asked him, eyes glowing with happiness despite the fatigue and discomfort he could see lurking there. "Wasn't it great?"

"What I think is that you're the most beautiful thing I've ever laid eyes on." Her expression softened as he took her face in his hand and brought his mouth down on hers. He nibbled at her luscious lower lip for a moment before delving his tongue inside to stroke hers, unable to get enough of her.

"I can see you two necking over there," said a scratchy voice from behind them. "Don't make me come over there and slap you for public indecency, Ryan, because I will if I have to."

Breaking the kiss, Ryan sighed and rested his forehead against Candace's. "She's like a bad smell that won't go away."

Candace giggled and wound her right arm around his waist. "Don't let her hear you say that."

Not in a million years.

Straightening, he turned slightly to face Ruby, who stood near the front entrance of the main building in her bright purple dress, puffing on a cigarette, her right wrist still wrapped up. "And here I thought you had to be all slapped out after last night."

Ruby exhaled a mouthful of smoke and grinned, her expression delighted as she dropped the cigarette and crushed it into the grass beneath the toe of her high-heeled shoe. "Not quite." Chuckling to herself, she turned and disappeared back inside.

He looked back at his wife. "I guess this means we're finally buddies?"

"I think it must," she answered, sounding impressed.

"Guess being teammates on a little covert night op is all it takes to win her over. Who knew?" Candace's husky laugh filled him with warmth. Slipping a hand around the nape of her neck, he kissed the tip of her nose. "I love you so much. More than you'll ever know. And I'll even risk bodily harm by dancing with your bat shit-crazy grandma later on to prove it."

She laughed again, softly this time, leaning her body against his. "She's in her late eighties, Ryan. Chances are she won't be around that much longer. We should embrace her quirkiness and enjoy her while we can."

More like she'll live to be over a hundred with the way she'd already pickled her internal organs with a lifetime of rye. "Like I said before," he said, wrapping his left arm around her waist to escort her back inside. He'd do anything for her. "She's growing on me."

Epilogue

Eight days later

"Okay, Maya and Jackson were right. This place really is paradise on earth."

Candace turned her head on the chaise lounge to look at Ryan, also stretched out on his back, enjoying the warm, tropical sun from the privacy of the back lawn of the beach house they'd rented in Poipu, on the island of Kauai.

The private property was a luxurious and insanely expensive accommodation that they were loving way too much. It wasn't something they ever would have shelled out for with their finances, but given everything that had happened at the resort, her grandmother had insisted upon paying for their second honeymoon, and for once, Ryan had accepted her generosity.

"I know," she murmured, basking in the heavenly combination of the warm sun and balmy breeze that rustled through the coconut palms ringing the sides of the yard and the birds of paradise that grew along the stone foundation of the house.

"Remind me to thank your grandma again when we get home."

She laughed at him. "Whatever, like you haven't already talked to her twice a day since we got here. I know you guys are texting buddies now."

Ryan's lips twitched, his eyes hidden by his shades. "I think I've grown on her."

"I think so too. Never in a million years would I have ever

thought you two would wind up bonding so tight."

"Seriously. I'd have taken her on a mission a year ago if I'd known that was the key."

Chuckling under her breath, she settled back against the padded headrest and let out a contented sigh. Before them, the endless blue of the Pacific Ocean stretched out, ending in turquoise waves that exploded into white foam as they crashed against the lava rock on the shore. "We stopping by that acai bowl place on the way back from the clinic?" They had to get their stitches out.

"Heck yeah. I love those things."

She picked up her phone, checked the time. "We'd better leave in ten minutes or so."

He grunted, appearing in no hurry to ever move again. She didn't blame him. This time away together was exactly what they'd both needed. His right hand and arm were a little swollen, and he still had some numbness and reduced grip strength. The doctors thought he'd get most of it back though.

Things had changed so much for them since the wedding last week. She'd officially become a civilian again as of two days ago, and it felt fantastic. She had several irons in the fire as far as job applications were concerned, all private sector, but one she had her fingers and toes crossed for. Ryan planned to stay in the Air Force for at least another few years, but for the next three months at least, he was all hers.

A lot more had happened over the past week as well.

The media had thankfully lost interest in her story and what happened at the resort, except to report about Eric March's legal case. He was currently in prison awaiting trial for charges that would either keep him locked up for the rest of his days, or the death penalty now that the government had uncovered everything he'd been planning. The majority of his followers had been tracked down and charged with various crimes.

Her phone rang in her hand. She lifted it, her heart jolting when she saw the number on display. Sitting up straight, she answered. "Hello?"

"Hi, Candace? It's Khalia Phillips, from Scottie's Foundation."

"Yes, hi." Her heart beat faster, excitement coursing through her. She'd been hoping and praying…

"We reviewed your application package, and I have to say, it's most impressive. I'll be in D.C. late next week and I'd love to interview you in person then, if that's convenient."

"Would Sunday work? I'm out of town on holiday until next Saturday." If not, she'd change her flight.

"Of course, that sounds fine, and considering recent events in Montana that I read about, I want you to enjoy every moment of your holiday."

Khalia must have looked her up online to do some research. "Yes, it's been nice to get away."

"I know exactly how that feels, and as a fellow survivor of traumatic events, I kind of feel like I know you already. So let's get in touch next week and figure out the details. Sound good?"

"Sounds *great.*"

"I should also tell you that we've already narrowed it down to you and one other applicant for this full-time position. But between you and me, you've got the edge over the other person." There was a smile in her voice, and Candace couldn't help but like her already. Everything she'd read about Khalia Phillips—formerly Khalia Patterson—was impressive.

"Well, thank you."

"You're welcome. I'll talk to you next week then, and can't wait to meet you. Enjoy your holiday. Bye."

"Bye." Ending the call, she whipped off her sunglasses and turned to face Ryan. "It was her! Khalia Phillips, with Scottie's Foundation."

He was turned onto his side facing her, his weight propped up by his left forearm, a big grin on his face. "And?"

"And she wants to interview me next Sunday. She basically said I've got better than a fifty percent shot at the job." She bit her lip, let out a little squeal.

"Congrats," he murmured, reaching across to capture her nape with his hand and drag her forward into a slow kiss. "I know you'll get it."

"I hope so." The job was everything she wanted. Flexible hours, she could do most of the work from home, and best of all, she'd be earning a living by helping fellow vets transition back into civilian life. "God, I'm so excited." She bounced on the chair. "Come on, let's get our stitches dealt with so we can go out and celebrate."

Rejuvenated and full of anticipation, she slid the glass door open and crossed the glossy teak floor from the living room past the deluxe, gourmet kitchen to the hallway. In the master suite located on the far end, she walked through into the attached bathroom and stripped off her bikini. She didn't consider her body bikini material but Ryan loved seeing her in it, so she'd worn it for him.

She was reaching for the dress she'd hung on the shower door when he came into the bathroom and stepped up behind her.

Facing the mirror, she had a perfect view of his thick, strong arms as they wound around her naked waist. "You should never get dressed again," he murmured against her ear, the rasp of his stubble making her shiver.

"Pervert."

"Can't help it. You're just so damn sexy; it's a crime to cover up these curves." He slid his hands up to cup her breasts and she swatted his forearm. The man had a one-track mind.

"None of that. We have stitches to get out, then champagne and lobster to find. And I should probably refill my birth control prescription too."

Chin nestled on her shoulder, he reached past her to pick up the compact holding her dwindling supply of birth control pills. "How many days you have left on this one?"

"Three. So I definitely need to get more while we're at the clinic. Especially since you want me naked all the time and can't seem to keep your hands—and other body parts—to yourself around me." She wiggled her bottom against the erection tenting the front of his swim shorts.

He met her gaze in the mirror, and her heart did a somersault. One look from him with those sexy mahogany-brown eyes and she just melted inside. "You complaining?"

"No." Not at all.

He set the pills down on the vanity, and, still staring into her eyes, wrapped his arms back around her middle. "What if you didn't refill the prescription?" he murmured.

She stilled as his meaning sank in, and her heart rate kicked up a notch. "Are you...sure?" Last week it had sounded as though the idea of starting a family was at least a few years away for him.

He gave a tiny nod, his chin rubbing against her shoulder. "Yeah. I've been thinking about it a lot since the wedding. These things can take a while sometimes, right? Who knows how long it'll take for us, and now that you're a civilian again, there's no reason to wait."

"But I might be starting a new job in another few weeks."

"Yeah, and you already told me you could work from home most of the time. We'd work it out."

A tremulous smile pulled at her mouth. She was so ready to try for a baby. She bit her lip, excitement fizzing through her veins. "I'm not even close to thirty-five yet."

"Mmm, but just think of all those perfectly good eggs going to waste right now." He rubbed his wide, warm palm over her lower abdomen, the protective, possessive gesture sending a thrill through her. "Although to be honest, I hope it doesn't happen too soon. I'm really looking forward to the trying part." He waggled his eyebrows.

She gave him a wry look. "Well then, let's hope your fast-movers miss the first few targets you lase, huh?"

A laugh burst out of him as she threw his words to Cam last week back in his face. He took her by the shoulders to spin her around, then framed her face between his hands, his thumbs caressing the tops of her cheekbones. "You're so the shit, Ace. I love you."

"I love you back." Smiling against his mouth, she sank into the kiss, into his embrace.

This new chapter of their lives was already off to a thrilling—if a little terrifying—start. She couldn't wait to find out what exciting possibilities the future had in store for them.

—The End—

* * * *

Thank you for reading NEVER SURRENDER. I really hope you enjoyed it and that you'll consider leaving a review at one of your favorite online retailers. It's a great way to help other readers discover new books.

If you liked NEVER SURRENDER and if don't want to miss any future releases, please join my newsletter. Direct link: http://kayleacross.com/v2/newsletter/

Discover the Liliana Hart MacKenzie Family Collection

Go to www.1001DarkNights.com for more information.

Spies & Stilettos by Liliana Hart
Trouble Maker by Liliana Hart
Rush by Robin Covington
Never Surrender by Kaylea Cross
Avenged by Jay Crownover
Bullet Proof by Avery Flynn
Delta: Rescue by Cristin Harber
Hot Witness by Lynn Raye Harris
Deep Trouble by Kimberly Kincaid
Wicked Hot by Gennita Low
Desire & Ice by Christopher Rice
Hollow Point by Lili St. Germain

Discover the World of 1001 Dark Nights

Collection One

Collection Two

Collection Three

Collection Four

Bundles

Discovery Authors

Blue Box Specials

Rising Storm

Liliana Hart's MacKenzie Family

About Kaylea Cross

NY Times and USA Today Bestselling author Kaylea Cross writes edge-of-your-seat military romantic suspense. Her work has won many awards and has been nominated for both the Daphne du Maurier and the National Readers' Choice Awards. A Registered Massage Therapist by trade, Kaylea is also an avid gardener, artist, Civil War buff, Special Ops aficionado, belly dance enthusiast, and former nationally-carded softball pitcher. She lives in Vancouver, BC, with her husband and family.

You can visit Kaylea at www.kayleacross.com. If you would like to be notified of future releases, please join her newsletter. Direct link: http://kayleacross.com/v2/newsletter/

Fast Kill

DEA FAST Series Book #3
By Kaylea Cross
Coming late April, 2017
Go to kayleacross.com for more information.

Wearing a pair of snug jeans and a feminine black-and-white polka-dot top with cap sleeves, Taylor exited the bathroom to find Logan on the couch with his left leg propped up, watching TV.

He looked over his shoulder at her and smiled a little, his hot gaze raking over the length of her body in a way that make her feel naked. Her bare toes curled into the carpet.

"My turn," he said as he got up.

"Your turn?" she mumbled, her mind going blank as all six-foot-plus of sexy alpha male prowled toward her.

He stopped a half-step away from her, a sensual smile tugging at the corners of his mouth. "For a shower," he murmured, then kissed her softly.

"Oh." Her eyelids fluttered as a delicious languor pervaded her body. Then he raised his head, gave her another of those knee-weakening smiles, and disappeared into the bathroom.

Taylor stared at the closed door, her skin tingling all over and her pulse thudding in her ears as the hiss of water started up in the shower. She wanted him. Why was she still standing here?

You are worthy.

Refusing to get lost in her head and ruin the moment by overthinking it, she walked over and grasped the doorknob. It turned easily under her hand, releasing a cloud of steam as she eased the door open.

At the sight before her, her lower belly did a slow, delicious somersault.

Logan stood under the spray facing away from her, the broad expanse of his muscled back and shoulders on display above the tiled half wall of the shower. His head was tipped back, the muscles in his arms and back flexing as he ran his hands through his wet hair.

Oh my God…

Her mouth went dry as she devoured the sight of him with her eyes.

He stilled, as though he sensed he was no longer alone. Lowering his hands, he half-turned to look at her. Taylor couldn't breathe, couldn't look away as their gazes connected and locked. He stood absolutely motionless while the water cascaded over his naked skin, watching her.

Waiting to see what she'd do.

On behalf of 1001 Dark Nights,
Liz Berry and M.J. Rose would like to thank ~

Liliana Hart
Scott Silverii
Steve Berry
Doug Scofield
Kim Guidroz
Jillian Stein
InkSlinger PR
Asha Hossain
Fedora Chen
Kasi Alexander
Pamela Jamison
Chris Graham
Jessica Johns
Dylan Stockton
and Simon Lipskar

Made in the USA
San Bernardino, CA
15 November 2017